GRAIL
OF
STARS

PENDRAGON LEGACY
BOOK 4

GRAIL OF STARS

KATHERINE ROBERTS

templar

A TEMPLAR BOOK

First published in the UK in 2013 by Templar Publishing,
an imprint of The Templar Company Limited,
Deepdene Lodge, Deepdene Avenue,
Dorking, Surrey, RH5 4AT, UK
www.templarco.co.uk

First UK edition

1 3 5 7 9 10 8 6 4 2

ISBN 978-1-84877-853-5

Printed and bound in Great Britain by
CPI Group (UK) Ltd, Croydon, CR0 4YY

For everyone on a Quest

Contents

Characters

ALBA – Rhianna's mist horse, a white mare
from Avalon.

ARIANRHOD – Rhianna's maid, ex-maid of
Morgan Le Fay. Her cheek bears a scar
in the shape of a pentacle.

CAI – young squire at Camelot who becomes
Rhianna's champion.

CHIEF CYNRIC – leader of the Saxons.

ELPHIN – Prince of Avalon and only son of
Lord Avallach.

EVENSTAR – Elphin's mist horse, a white
stallion from Avalon.

GARETH – older squire, Cai's rival.

KING ARTHUR – king of Britain. His ghost
appears to Rhianna while his body
sleeps in Avalon awaiting rebirth.

LADY ELAINE – Sir Lancelot's wife and Sir
Galahad's mother. She was once

a Grail maiden and now lives in the
Grail Castle.

LORD AVALLACH – Lord of Avalon and
Elphin's father. Leader of the Wild
Hunt.

MERLIN – King Arthur's druid. Morgan Le
Fay drowned his man's body but his
spirit lives in the body of a merlin
falcon. He can still work magic.

MORDRED – Rhianna's cousin and rival for
the throne; the son of Morgan Le Fay.

MORGAN LE FAY – Mordred's mother, and
Arthur's sister, a witch. Now dead, her
spirit advises Mordred from Annwn.

NIMUE – the Lady of the Lake, who took
King Arthur's sword Excalibur after
Arthur's death and gave it to Rhianna.

QUEEN GUINEVERE – Rhianna's mother.

RHIANNA PENDRAGON – daughter of King
Arthur, raised in Avalon.

SANDY – Cai's pony, rescued from the Saxons.

SIR AGRAVAINE – grumpy older knight.

SIR BEDIVERE – a young knight, also known as 'Soft Hands' because of his gentle nature.

SIR BORS – leader of King Arthur's knights.

SIR GALAHAD – Sir Lancelot's son. He died on his quest after finding the Grail.

SIR LANCELOT – Arthur's champion knight, whose love for Queen Guinevere caused him to break the Lance of Truth when he fought against his king.

SIR PERCIVAL – Sir Galahad's best friend.

THE FISHER KING – lord of the Grail Castle, where the Grail of Stars is kept safe

THE SHADRAKE – a dragon from Annwn, breathes ice instead of fire and hunts between worlds.

UTHER PENDRAGON – father of King Arthur and Morgan Le Fay. Now dead, his spirit lives in Annwn.

To Dragon Land

Druid
Beacon

Lonely Tor
[Glastonbury]

SUMMER SEA

Marshes

Stone
Circle

To Mines of
Lyonesse

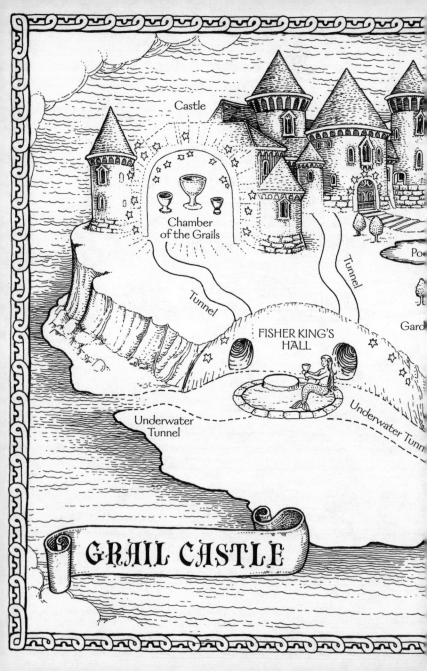

Castle

Chamber
of the Grails

Tunnel

Tunnel

FISHER KING'S
HALL

Po

Gard

Underwater
Tunnel

Underwater Tunn

GRAIL CASTLE

Cove
(where mist
horses hide)

Pool

Pool

Enchanted
Mists

Harbour

Ship of
Ghosts

Enchanted
Mists

Four lights stand against the dark:
The Sword Excalibur that was
forged in Avalon,
The Lance of Truth made by the
hands of men,
The Crown of Dreams, which hides
the jewel of Annwn,
And the Grail said to hold all the
stars in heaven.

Dark Tor

As the boat neared the island gateway to Avalon, Mordred's right hand tingled – the only part of him that could feel pain these days. He pulled a black gauntlet over the rotting fingers and signalled Uther Pendragon's ghostly army to surround the shore.

"Faster!" he growled to his bloodbeards. "We don't want anyone getting away."

The men glanced uneasily at the ghosts in the mist and bent over their oars. The boat crunched on the shingle near a small village. Dark wings blotted out the stars above the

Lonely Tor. Mordred grinned as screams came out of the night. The shadrake had done its work well.

Mordred seized his axe and jumped ashore. He watched the monks run out of their church and down the hill towards the village, tripping over their robes in their panic. His lip curled – unarmed followers of the Christ God, who thought they were safe on their little island under Camelot's protection.

He nodded to his men, and the bloodbeards threw flaming torches into the huts. There were more screams as the monks' families ran out towards the water, then ran back again when they saw Uther's dead warriors riding out of the mist.

Trapped between the ghosts and the flames, the people huddled together on the beach, clutching their children and sobbing as their homes burned. Mordred ordered his bloodbeards to drag their leader to him. They flung the old man to his knees in the sand. The monk crossed himself.

Mordred laughed. "Do you know who I am?"

"N-no, sir," the monk stammered.

Mordred gave him a frustrated look. He must have made himself too handsome when he grew his new body from his decaying mortal fist. Then a lanky, dark-haired boy yelled from the crowd, "I know you… you're Prince Mordred!"

The lad looked vaguely familiar, but Mordred couldn't think where he'd seen him before until a woman said, "Hush, Gareth. I thought you told us Mordred was dead?"

Mordred chuckled as he remembered the squire who had tried to kill him at the gates of Camelot last year. The boy did not have his bow and arrows today.

"Prince Mordred!" The monk looked at him more closely. "We heard they burned your body at Camelot… Are you a ghost?" He glanced uncertainly at Uther's horsemen out in the mist.

"Is this the hand of a ghost?" Mordred clutched the old man's throat with his black gauntlet and squeezed until rotten flesh leaked out of the glove. He laughed again. "I'm the rightful heir to the throne, and I don't intend to die before I sit on it. Now tell me, wise one. How do we get from here to Avalon?"

"I d-don't know," the monk whispered.

"This is a holy place now. Lord Avallach's Wild Hunt does not ride this way any more."

Mordred sighed. "I can see we'll have to do this the hard way." He motioned with his axe, and his bloodbeards grabbed Gareth from the cowering huddle of villagers. The squire reached for his dagger, but Mordred knocked it out of his hand. "Drown the Camelot brat," he ordered.

The bloodbeards dragged the struggling boy to the water and pushed his head under. Bubbles came up as Gareth thrashed and kicked. Then his body went limp and floated face down. His mother screamed and splashed in to rescue it, sobbing, "My son... you've killed my son!"

"If I have to, I'll drown every living soul on this island. Starting with the youngest,"

Mordred said. "That means you'll be the last to die, old man. Tell me the way to Avalon now, and you'll save your people a lot of grief."

Tears sprang to the old monk's eyes. "I'm begging you, sir prince! Leave us in peace. We have nothing of value here. We're simple folk. If you want to know how to get to the fairy isle, you should ask a druid. Merlin used to come this way... he rowed his boat into the mist and vanished... that's all I know, I swear it in the name of our Lord!"

The old man was choking. Mordred let him go.

He flexed his stiff fingers thoughtfully. In this place, Uther's warriors were only faintly visible where the starlight touched them. They couldn't come to Avalon with him, because their souls belonged in Annwn now.

But they could catch anyone coming through these mists from the mainland.

He smiled. "I just might do that. My cousin Rhianna will be heading this way soon with her friends. I'm going to need somewhere to stay until she gets here."

He looked up at the Tor. The shadrake perched on the roof of the church, lashing its tail. Purple lightning crackled around the tower, reminding him of when his mother, Morgan Le Fay, had ambushed Merlin as the druid brought his cousin through the mists from Avalon.

He pointed to the church. "That'll do nicely."

The monk frowned. "But sir, that's our holy place! Queen Guinevere built it for us because the Grail was once hidden in a cave up there."

"Then it's perfect," Mordred said. "I'm sure

my aunt won't mind. My hand pains me.
I'll need one of your herbal cures, and I'll
need someone to serve me." His eye fell on
Gareth's weeping mother. "You, woman, stop
snivelling! Your boy was a squire of Camelot,
which is why I had to get rid of him. I don't
want news of my resurrection leaking back to
Arthur's knights before I'm ready. My men
will take his body back to the mainland and
make it look like an accident, so he'll get a
burial, if that's what you're worried about.
Now, get up there and make the place ready
for me."

The woman raised her tear-stained face
and hissed, "Ready for you? I'll kill you first!"
She snatched the bloodbeard captain's spear
from the rock where he'd propped it while
he drowned her son, and launched it with

unexpected accuracy at Mordred.

Mordred spread his arms wide and laughed as the spear entered the place where his heart should be. The shaft tickled as it passed through his shadow-body. He spun round to see it land, shivering, in the sand behind him.

Everyone stared at him in fear. The monk crossed himself again. The bloodbeards grinned. Gareth's mother fell to her knees, trembling.

Mordred retrieved the spear and raised his voice. "You'll find it harder to kill me than you think. King Arthur didn't manage it at Camlann, his daughter Rhianna didn't manage it when she rode out of Avalon, and his knights didn't manage it with their fire." His tone hardened and he poked the terrified woman in the stomach. "But if any of you try something stupid like that again, I'll drown another child for every attempt on my life. And if anyone is thinking of leaving this island without my permission, Uther's army of ghosts out there will take your souls straight to Annwn. Understand?"

The islanders nodded. Only the crackle of flames broke the silence.

Mordred smiled. "Good. Then there's no need for further demonstrations. You'd better get to work if you want to save those huts. I'm sure your God won't mind if you use one of them to pray in while I'm staying in your church. Carry on as normal. And when Princess Rhianna arrives, send her up to me. Then we'll head on over to Avalon and leave you in peace. Her fairy friend will know how to get home, if the druid won't tell me the way."

Secrets

Enchantments cloaked the Lonely Tor
When a squire drowned on mist-bound shore,
While a damsel searched to no avail
For secrets of the missing Grail.

The stables at Camelot were quiet after lunch, with the horses settled for the afternoon. Rhianna slipped into her mist horse's stall and patted the white mare she had ridden from Avalon two years ago. "Keep watch, Alba," she whispered. "I'm going to wear my crown for a bit."

The little horse snorted, pleased to see her mistress but disappointed Rhianna had brought the Pendragon crown instead of an apple. *I cannot eat jewels*, she complained.

Rhianna smiled. "I know you can't, my darling. But these are magic jewels. They'll show me where to find the Grail of Stars, and then I can take you home." Taking a deep breath, she jammed the Crown over her unruly copper hair.

"Help me, Father," she whispered. "Where should I look?"

She felt a warm spot at the back of her head, where the jewel containing King Arthur's secrets had been restored to the third Light after they'd got it back from her evil cousin Mordred last year. She closed her eyes, hoping the magic would show her something useful this time. A thick green mist surrounded her. She glimpsed shapes moving inside it and spent a frustrating time trying to follow them. Then the Crown became hot, and her spirit left her body.

❧

She was flying over water. She heard the creak of wood as a ghostly ship appeared from the mist below. It had white sails and shone like a star. A tall, slender knight with golden hair knelt over a boy's shivering body in the stern, holding something in his hands that lit up the deck.

"Wait!" she called. "Is that the Grail…?"

But already the ship was sailing away into the mist. She tried to follow it, but the green clouds thickened again. Flying blind, she lost all sense of time.

Then a lone hill loomed ahead with purple lightning flashing around a building with a black tower. Screams came from below, and suddenly she was falling. Her spirit spun helplessly down towards the ghostly green sea. She could not see, could not breathe. Icy water closed over her head, and she heard her cousin Mordred laughing.

⚜

"Rhia! Wake up now, Rhianna Pendragon!"

The tinkle of an Avalonian harp banished the vision. She gasped for air and struck out at the hands trying to hold her down.

"Ow!" someone muttered. "I think she's still dreaming."

"No, she's back with us." That was her friend Prince Elphin's voice, quiet but tense. "Get the Crown off her. Careful."

Something caught in her hair, and Rhianna grabbed for it. Her hand closed about an unexpectedly hot jewel. She sucked in her breath and let go.

"That's right," Elphin continued. "You take it, Arianrhod. Wrap it up in something."

Rhianna felt water drip on her leg and remembered her vision. "Mordred...!" she gasped.

The harp rippled again, and Elphin's voice filled with magic. "This is Camelot, Rhia," he sang. "You're safe now. Prince Mordred's dead, remember? He can't hurt you unless you invite his ghost in here."

A shudder went through her. *Ghosts, that's*

all I saw. Warmth returned to her body, and the icy water became a puddle of wet straw. She brushed it off with a grimace and opened her eyes.

She was lying in a corner of Alba's stall. It was dark outside. A single torch burned in the passage.

Three anxious faces peered down at her. Plump, fair-haired Cai, who was a knight now but still slept in the squires' dormitory; her maid Arianrhod, whose dark hair covered the pentacle scar Morgan Le Fay had cut into her cheek; and Prince Elphin, with his violet eyes and extra Avalonian fingers. Her mist horse's nose pushed between them.

You were making a lot of noise, Alba scolded. *And you spilled my water! I told Evenstar to bring his rider.*

It was such a relief to be safe with her friends that Rhianna laughed. She sat up and threw handfuls of wet straw at them. "Back off," she said. "I can hardly breathe with you three staring at me like that."

Cai grinned. "She's all right!" he said, sounding relieved too. "Why are you sleeping in the stables, Damsel Rhia? Aren't your rooms in the Damsel Tower good enough for the daughter of King Arthur?"

She pulled a face. "I wanted to be alone, and this is about the only place I can get any peace these days – until my horse decided to tell everyone where I am, that is." She met Elphin's whirling purple gaze. "You didn't have to wake the others. If Cai's here, the whole of Camelot will know where to find me by morning. Mordred's ghost, too, no doubt."

Her friend lowered his harp and frowned. "That's not funny, Rhia! It took me ages to call your spirit back this time. And it is morning, nearly. What were you doing wearing the Crown of Dreams in the stables anyway?"

"Using it to look for the Grail of Stars, of course," Rhianna said. "I saw a ship in the mist with a knight and a boy on board. The knight was holding something bright, but I couldn't see what. When I tried to follow the ship I saw an island in the mist, and then I heard Mordred laughing…" She frowned and rubbed her head in memory. "Is the Crown all right? Let me see." She lurched to her feet, but only managed two steps across the stall before her knees buckled. She sat down again in the puddle, dizzy

Elphin shook his head and knelt at her side. "Take it slowly, Rhia," he said. He glanced up at Cai. "See if you can find her something to eat. She's missed supper, if Arianrhod's right."

"I thought she was having supper with her mother," Arianrhod said. The maid hung back in the shadows, keeping the third Light wrapped in her cloak.

"The queen always eats with Sir Lancelot in the evenings, you know that," Rhianna said with a scowl. "And stop treating me as if I'm sick! I'm just a bit dizzy from using the magic, that's all. I'll be fine in a moment."

Elphin's harp tinkled again, soothing her bad temper. But she caught his wrist to silence the strings. "Enough, Prince Elphin!" she said, trying to force lightness into her voice. "I don't want to fall asleep again. I've already spent most of a day and night wearing the Crown of Dreams."

She lifted his hand and examined his slender fingers for blisters. She knew what it must have cost him to play his harp in the presence of the third Light. At least there was no blood this time. She let go of his hand and smiled. "Thank you."

Elphin pressed his lips together as he bagged his harp. "You should be more careful. Don't forget that crown killed Lady Morgan and Mordred."

"It won't kill me. I'm heir to the Pendragon throne."

"What did the knight on the ship look like, Damsel Rhianna?" Cai asked, returning with a bucket of bruised apples they kept in the stables for the horses. "He might be one of the knights who died on a Grail Quest."

Rhianna tried to remember. "Young,

I think… I couldn't see his face, but he was tall and slim… and he had golden hair."

"Could be Sir Percival or Sir Galahad," Cai said doubtfully. "The boy you saw on the ship was probably his squire – none of them came back. Did you see Mordred's ghost too?"

"No," Rhianna said with a frown. "I just heard him laughing… but that was probably one of my own memories from last year. I think the shadrake was part of the vision too. That crown's as bad as Merlin – it never shows me anything useful!" She shook her head in frustration. A whole winter of wearing the third Light, with its secrets of the Pendragons stretching back to the ancient Dragonlords, and the only thing she'd seen clearly was a ghostly knight on a ship!

Elphin smiled. "Father once told me it

doesn't matter how much someone knows. You have to know what questions to ask."

"I know what questions to ask it!" Rhianna said, scowling at him. "I want to know where the Grail of Stars is so I can take the four Lights back to Avalon to wake my father, but all I've seen so far is water and mist!"

"Maybe the Grail's in the lake where you found Excalibur?" Cai suggested, munching one of the apples he'd found. "That's usually misty."

"Or across the sea?" Arianrhod ventured. "Where the Romans live? That might be why you saw a ship?"

"They don't have mist in Rome, silly," Cai said. "Too hot. If it's across the sea, it's more likely to be in Dragonland, like the Crown was."

"I hope we don't have to go back there," Arianrhod whispered, hugging the cloak-wrapped crown. "That's the gateway to Annwn!"

"You weren't even with us in Dragonland," Cai pointed out. "You were safe here at Camelot with Gareth. I was the one who had to fight dragons and rescue Damsel Rhianna from the shadrake's lair! Good thing I was carrying the Lance of Truth, that's all I can say."

"And who rescued you *and* the Lance from the shadrake?" Rhianna reminded the boy with a smile.

The very thought of Dragonland, where Mordred had tried to bury her in the shadrake's lair, made Rhianna break into a cold sweat. But if the Grail did turn out to be in Dragonland, she'd have to swallow her fears and go back. At least her cousin wouldn't be there this time, and the roads were safe now. Gareth, the older squire who had helped them defeat Mordred last year, had even been allowed to ride out by himself to visit his family on the Lonely Tor.

But Cai's words made her think. Nimue's lake…? Could the Grail be so close to Camelot? What if someone had thrown the fourth Light into the lake as an offering to the fish-lady Nimue, as the knights had done with Excalibur after King Arthur died? That might be why nobody could find it.

Shouts from outside interrupted them, followed by an urgent pounding at the gates. The horses pricked their ears and whinnied, hoping for breakfast.

Rhianna got to her feet, more carefully this time, and fed Alba her apple core. "Something's going on out there," she said, taking the crown from Arianrhod. "We'd better get back into the castle."

❧

By the time they reached the courtyard, the big gates of Camelot had opened. A troop of shaggy Saxon ponies trotted through, led by a big man with yellow braids. One of the ponies had a dripping bundle tied across its back. A sentry ran into the castle, shouting for the knights. Sir Lancelot hurried out, strapping on his sword.

Rhianna's heart beat faster at the sight of the Saxons. "It's Chief Cynric!" she said, thrusting the crown back into Arianrhod's hands. "Take this up to my room and get breakfast ready. I'm going to find out what's happened."

Arianrhod shook her head. "I don't think

that's a very good idea, Lady Rhia, not with your dress all dirty like that. What if your mother sees you?"

Rhianna looked down at her skirt, which had picked up a big green stain from the stables. It smelled of horse. "Don't fuss, Arianrhod," she said. "The queen's still in bed, and the knights are used to seeing me looking scruffy."

She led her friends across the courtyard. A ring of curious squires had gathered around the ponies. The dripping bundle appeared to be a body, hanging facedown. Sir Lancelot examined it, while a bleary-eyed Sir Bedivere and Sir Bors emerged to join him and spread their arms to keep the boys away. "Stay back!" Sir Bors ordered gruffly. "Get on with your work. There's horses waiting to be fed and mucked out."

The squires reluctantly went off to the stables, casting glances over their shoulders. They seemed subdued.

"It's Gareth!" Cai said, his eyes going wide as Sir Lancelot lifted the dead boy's head. "Looks like they fished him out of the river."

Sir Lancelot let the boy's head drop. "Drowned," he muttered.

A shiver crept down Rhianna's spine as she remembered the boy she'd seen on the ghostly ship in her vision. Elphin's eyes deepened to purple, and he gave her a worried look. His hand tightened on his harp.

"Been attacked, more like, goin' by them bruises on his arms," Sir Bors growled.

Sir Lancelot was now questioning the Saxons, who shook their heads. He frowned and glanced up at the queen's window. Then he spotted Rhianna and her friends watching and muttered something to Sir Bedivere, who came over to join them.

"The Saxons found his body under the bridge," the knight explained gently. "Must have been on his way back to Camelot when robbers jumped him then dumped his body in the river, poor lad – his dagger's gone, and there's no sign of his pony."

They stared at each other. Cai bit his lip. Arianrhod glanced nervously at the open gates.

"Bloodbeards?" Rhianna demanded.

Sir Bedivere sighed. "We don't know yet, but we'll find out. Lancelot's called a meeting of the Round Table. Damsel Rhianna, will you run up and tell your mother? And remember, young knight…" He fixed Cai with a stern look. "This is Round Table business now, so don't go spreading it about that we think Gareth was attacked on the road. We had quite enough of that kind of thing when Prince Mordred was alive."

◄ 2 ►

Sir Galahad's Ghost

At the Table Round the knights sat down
To right the wrong done to the crown.
When Rhianna raised her sword to call
Young Galahad from his ghostly hall.

On their way back up the winding stair
of the Damsel Tower, Rhianna told
Arianrhod to unwrap the Crown so she could

check it for damage. It had cooled, and the magic jewels containing the secrets of the Pendragons looked dull. Even the powerful jewel of Annwn that contained the secret of dragon riding felt cold.

They paused at one of the narrow windows. Beyond the river, Rhianna could just make out the Lonely Tor rising from the marshes where she and Elphin had ridden through the mists from Avalon two years ago. A black cloud hung over the lone hill, and lightning flashed on the horizon, reminding her of her vision. She shivered. It had felt a bit like she was spirit-riding the shadrake at one point, except she couldn't have been, because the dragon had gone back to Annwn when they'd burned the dark knight's body last year.

Arianrhod tugged at her sleeve. "Did you

ask the Crown about my parents, Lady Rhia?"
she whispered.

Rhianna frowned at the girl's hopeful face.
"Oh, Arianrhod, I completely forgot! I'll ask it
next time, I promise."

They knew now that Arianrhod's mother
had been a Grail maiden, who had left her baby
on the hill outside Camelot for the knights to
find, but they still didn't know who her father
had been.

The maid lowered her eyes. "It doesn't
matter," she said. "You've got more important
things to do, I know that."

"It *does* matter. It's important to you."

Rhianna knew exactly what it felt like to
grow up not knowing who your parents are. Her
own childhood had been spent with Elphin's
family, beyond the mists in Avalon. The first

time she'd seen her father, he had been lying in the bottom of Merlin's boat after Mordred had killed him in battle. She wished his ghost would appear so she could ask him about the ship she'd seen in the mist. But she hadn't seen the king's soul since the night they had burned Mordred.

"We'll talk about it after the meeting," she promised. "Can you go and wake the queen for me? I've got to get changed."

She hurried up the stairs to her room and tossed the Crown on to her bed, then stripped off her soiled dress and threw it on top. Quickly, she pulled on her riding leggings and tunic. She fingered her Avalonian armour, but it seemed a bit much just for a meeting of the Round Table. Finally, she strapped on her sword belt and slipped Excalibur into its red scabbard. At once, she felt stronger.

She ran back down the tower stairs, excitement stirring her stomach. Although it was awful what had happened to Gareth, she was glad of the distraction. Things had been much too tame at Camelot since Mordred died.

The knights had been caught in bed by the Saxons' arrival. Some of them were entering the hall only half dressed, their tabards hanging loose. Others munched rolls snatched from the kitchens on their way. The smell of the freshly baked bread made Rhianna's stomach rumble.

"Here," Cai said, puffing as he joined her. He held out a honey cake, still warm from the oven. "You won't be much good in a battle if you don't eat."

"We already defeated Mordred's army," Rhianna reminded him, adding a cushion to her father's chair and placing Excalibur on the table before her. "So there won't be a battle. But whatever happened to Gareth, at least it's got the knights to call a meeting of the Round Table. Don't rush off afterwards. I've got an idea how to persuade them to let us go and look for the Grail." She bit into the cake and almost spat it out again. "That's hot! How come you don't burn your mouth?"

"Practice!" Cai grinned. "Quick, eat up! Here come Sir Lancelot and the queen."

The silver-haired knight strode in, talking urgently to Queen Guinevere. The queen's gaze swept around the table and caught Rhianna brushing crumbs from her legs. Guinevere's copper hair, bright as Rhianna's own, had been tamed in a jewelled net, and she wore a green and gold gown. She shook her head when she saw her daughter's riding leggings.

"You don't need to be here this morning, Rhianna darling," she said, waving at the knights to sit down. "Nor you, young Cai. This is a minor incident at my monastery. We just need to decide who's going to the Lonely Tor to investigate how such a tragic accident could happen."

Rhianna rested her hands on Excalibur, thinking uneasily of her vision. "And what if it wasn't an accident? Gareth had bruises on his neck."

The queen frowned. "How do you know that?"

"We saw him, of course—" Cai winced as Rhianna gave him a kick under the table.

"I mean, er, all the squires saw, Your Majesty. The Saxons arrived with his body just as we was starting the mucking out."

Guinevere grimaced at Sir Lancelot. "Can't keep anything from my daughter these days, it seems."

"She does wear the Pendragon crown, my lady." The silver-haired knight gave Rhianna an amused look.

Rhianna felt fairly certain her mother didn't know she'd spent the night in the stables, but she avoided Sir Lancelot's pale stare. It reminded her of the way Merlin used to look at her, before he'd lost his druid's body and transferred his spirit into the small falcon that bore the same name.

"Sir Lancelot?" Rhianna whispered, catching the knight's sleeve as he passed her chair. "I need to talk to you—"

"Hush, darling," Guinevere said as the doors boomed shut. "If you're determined to stay, don't interrupt. Cai, get back to your place. The meeting's about to start, and we don't want to be here all morning."

Cai hurried back to his seat, from where he made faces at Rhianna. She reluctantly settled back into her chair as Sir Lancelot addressed the knights.

"A squire drowned last night," he began. "He'd been visiting his family on the Lonely Tor. From the marks on his body, it looks like he'd been in a struggle. It's possible thieves attacked him on the road and dumped his body in the river afterwards, but as far as we know he wasn't carrying anything of value except his dagger. We'll send someone across to the Lonely Tor to investigate. It might have been an accident, but it's not the kind of thing Arthur would have allowed to happen in his kingdom. If people are not safe visiting our holy places, where can they be safe?"

"I'll go," Sir Bors volunteered, standing up with a scrape of his chair. "Bedivere can come with me to do the talking."

The knight everyone called 'Soft Hands' stood, too. He smiled at the queen. "Don't worry, my lady. We'll soon find out what happened to the poor lad."

"Best get going as soon as you can," Sir Lancelot said. "You can take some of the older squires with you. They were Gareth's friends, and it'll do them good to learn the less glamorous parts of the job before Arthur comes back to knight them." He exchanged a meaningful glance with the queen.

Cai looked expectantly at Rhianna. Every bone in her body wanted to stand up and volunteer to go with them. Anything to get out of Camelot after the long winter, and back in Alba's saddle galloping across the meadows bright with spring flowers. Instead, she sat very still, her hands clenched on Excalibur's scabbard. Gareth had never been a friend of hers, and the investigation might take ages. If she went with Sir Bors and Sir Bedivere to the Lonely Tor, that would delay her quest for the fourth Light.

"Damsel Rhianna?" Sir Bors said with a gruff cough. "A magic sword might be useful on this trip."

"And a magic lance!" Cai said, his eyes shining. "I can come too, can't I?"

Rhianna shook her head. "I've got more important things to do. I still need to find the Grail of Stars to bring my father back to Camelot. The Crown of Dreams sent me a vision last night. I saw an island that might have been the Lonely Tor, surrounded by green mist. Then I saw a ship sailing away from it with a knight and a shining light on board. I think it was the Grail, and I think my vision means we need to journey across the sea to get it back, but I'll need some knights to accompany me." She looked around the table, but they all avoided her gaze. Only Sir Bedivere would meet her eyes, and he shook his head.

The queen sighed. "Darling, be sensible. We've spoken about this already. None of Arthur's knights ever managed to bring the Grail to Camelot. I know you want your father back, but the knights need to investigate Squire Gareth's death. They haven't time at the moment to ride out on a quest based on a dream. Be patient."

"I've been patient all winter," Rhianna said, her blood rising. "I think you *want* me to fail my quest, so you can live happily ever after at Camelot with Sir Lancelot!"

Guinevere flushed, and Sir Lancelot scowled. The knights gave embarrassed coughs and pretended to be discussing her vision. But Rhianna knew they were listening to every word.

She gripped Excalibur's hilt harder. "Well it's true, isn't it, Mother?" she said, looking around the table for support. "You never really believed I would complete my quest for the four Lights. And now I've got three of them, you're afraid I might find the fourth and bring King Arthur back from Avalon to reclaim his throne. Then Sir Lancelot will have to leave again—"

She'd gone too far. The queen's hand shot out and slapped her across the cheek.

"That's enough, Rhianna!" she said, getting to her feet. "I'm not discussing this in here. Sir Bors and Sir Bedivere will take a party to the Tor and find out how the boy drowned. If Cai wants to go with them, he can – it'll help him learn to carry the Lance of Truth like a proper knight. And since you've made it quite clear you're much too busy to ride with them, you, *daughter*, will get changed into attire more suitable for a princess of Camelot and meet me in my rooms for lunch. We'll talk about this Grail Quest of yours further then."

Drawing her cloak around her, she walked

quickly from the hall with her head held high. The guards opened the doors to let her out.

Rhianna stared after her mother, her eyes filling with hot tears. The slap had not hurt very much – Guinevere did not have muscles from riding and fighting like she did. But the shame of it made Rhianna's cheeks burn. Her mother had struck her before the knights of the Round Table! Men she'd led to victory in battle against Mordred and his bloodbeards, and whose spirits were linked to her sword Excalibur.

"Well then, that seems to be decided," Sir Bedivere said, breaking the awkward silence. "Are you coming with us then, Cai? Best get packed if you are. We're riding out as soon as we're ready."

Cai cast Rhianna an anguished look. The knights all started talking at once. She heard her name mentioned and wanted to escape like her mother had and hide in Alba's stable.

But she had something to do first. She blinked away the tears, jumped up on her chair and drew Excalibur.

"We haven't finished," she said, pleased when her voice emerged steady and strong. "I can show you what the Crown showed me. Close the doors!"

Seeing the Sword of Light shining in her hand, the knights went quiet. The guards on the door glanced at Sir Lancelot, who gave Rhianna an irritated look.

"Close them," he said with a sigh. "The girl's going to try the magic anyway, and I'd rather we were all here with her when she does. Maybe she'll calm down afterwards and let us get on with the business of running a kingdom."

Everyone shifted in their seats and watched Rhianna warily.

"All right, get it over with," Lancelot muttered to her. "Though by the way you're acting this morning, you thoroughly deserved that slap. You seem to think your quest is all that matters, when we've still got Mordred's mess to clear up and a drowned squire to take care of, before any of us have time to go looking for things that don't belong in this world, like your Grail. I doubt you saw it in your vision, anyway. Nobody's seen the Grail since Arthur died."

"I *did* see it... I'll show you."

Rhianna stepped on to the Round Table and walked to the centre, where a slot waited for her sword beneath the opening in the roof. The druid symbols carved into the blue stone shimmered, and Excalibur's jewel brightened in response. She took a deep breath and lowered the enchanted blade into the table.

The knights peered warily into the shadows. Rhianna looked up at the hole in the roof, where the first rays of the morning sun pierced the hall. But they didn't reach as far as the Round Table, and no vision of the Grail came floating down on them, as the songs claimed had happened in King Arthur's day.

"Right," Sir Bors said. "At least that proves Damsel Rhianna's vision is nothing much to worry about. If we've finished, then maybe we can get going to the Tor—"

He broke off as the knights sucked in a collective breath. Rhianna smiled in triumph. The golden-haired ghostly knight from her vision sat in her chair with a shining light cupped between his hands, too bright to look at. She squinted at it through her fingers, but still couldn't see what he held.

"It's Sir Galahad!" Cai breathed.

The others all looked at Sir Lancelot, who was staring at the ghost.

"Galahad, my son…" he said in a choked voice. He reached across the table to touch the younger knight's arm, but his hand passed right through it.

"Hello, Father," the shining ghost said. He smiled and lifted his hands. "See, I told you I would find it."

Lancelot blinked at the ghostly knight's hands in confusion.

"You still can't see it, Father?" Galahad looked disappointed. He lifted the bright light to show the other knights. "Any of you?

Sir Bedivere? Sir Bors? Sir Agravaine? And who's that new young knight I see over there?" He peered across the Round Table at Cai.

"Sir Cai!" Cai said proudly. "I'm the Pendragon's champion now. I carry the Lance of Truth. Princess Rhianna knighted me last year."

The ghostly knight raised his gaze to Rhianna. "Ah, yes… we heard King Arthur's daughter had returned to Camelot. Seems your princess can see things the rest of you still have trouble believing in."

The living knights frowned at the ghost. "The lad ain't carrying nothing that I can see," Sir Bors muttered. "What can you see, Damsel Rhianna?"

"Not much!" Rhianna said in frustration. "It's too bright. Is that the Grail of Stars,

Sir Galahad? What does it look like? Can you put it down on the table a moment?"

She wished she could go over and get a proper look at what the ghostly knight held, but if she let go of Excalibur, the magic that had summoned Galahad's spirit to the Round Table would die.

Sir Galahad laughed. "Believe me, you don't want to find *this* Light, Princess."

"Yes I do!" Rhianna said, setting her jaw. "The three I have are not enough to restore my father's soul to his body, so I need the Grail as well. You know where it is, don't you? Tell me."

She gripped Excalibur's white jewel, willing the ghostly knight to answer.

"It's in my mother's castle," Sir Galahad said, frowning a little as the Sword's magic commanded him to speak the truth.

"Meet me at the lake, and I'll take you there."

"Which lake?"

"This is your quest, Princess, not mine." The ghost began to fade. "Mother sends her love," he added, opening his hands towards Sir Lancelot. Stars sparkled across the table between them.

"Wait!" Rhianna said. "Don't go…"

But Galahad had vanished, and the stars winked out too. She sheathed Excalibur in frustration and returned to her seat, placing the sword on the table while she checked her chair. The knights were whispering and casting sideways glances at Sir Lancelot. She heard the name 'Elaine' and 'Grail maiden'.

Her head spun.

"That's it!" she said, turning excitedly to Sir Lancelot. "Galahad's mother was a Grail maiden, wasn't she? That means you must have been to the Grail Castle too… so you can show me the way!"

Sir Lancelot's hand closed on her arm. "The meeting's over," he said, stopping her from sitting down. He swept Excalibur off the table and strode from the hall, dragging Rhianna with him.

❧

Sir Lancelot's grip on her wrist hurt. He carried Excalibur in its red scabbard in his other hand, out of her reach. Rhianna tried to pull free, but Lancelot was strong and she didn't want the other knights thinking he had surprised her. Bad enough that they had already seen her mother slap her.

She reminded the silver-haired knight that

she needed to change before having lunch with her mother. But he hustled her down some steps, into the nearest underground storeroom. He pushed her inside and kicked the door shut. Then he stood with his back to it and folded his arms.

Rhianna stumbled over a sack of apples and whirled to face him, angry and a little scared. The storeroom had no windows, just air holes in the door that turned Lancelot into a menacing silhouette. "Give me back my sword!" she said.

"No, Princess. Not until we've got this thing straight. I know Guinevere wants to talk to you about this quest of yours, but she's your mother and I know you don't listen to her. Since your father isn't here, maybe you'll listen to me. Sit."

Rhianna looked at the sacks and folded her arms, too.

"Have it your own way," Sir Lancelot said. "This won't take long. I expect you'll find out most of this from the Crown eventually, but it'll be a lot quicker if I tell you the truth now, so you don't get the wrong idea and go running around Camelot asking questions and upsetting your mother."

He took a deep breath. "Right, as you already know that ghost you summoned just now was my son, Galahad. It seems he actually found the Grail, the little idiot, but he didn't live to tell the tale. He dared to drink from it, and it killed him. His mother is the Lady Elaine..." He paused. "My wife. And before you ask, yes, she was a Grail maiden. Until Galahad came along, that is." He smiled ruefully. "That's why I married her, for the sake of her honour."

Rhianna forgot her anger and sat down on

a sack, confused. "But I thought you loved my mother?"

Lancelot grimaced. "I love the queen more than my own heart. But she was married to your father. For the sake of Guinevere's honour, I couldn't risk stealing so much as a kiss while Arthur lived. You have no idea how hard it was – I've told you before, I'm only human. I found happiness with Elaine."

She frowned at the knight. "So why did you leave your wife and return to Camelot?"

"I carried the Lance of Truth. I was the Pendragon's champion. Arthur needed me. Elaine understood, and she couldn't leave the Grail unprotected to come with me. But she let me take our son Galahad to Camelot so Arthur could make him a knight of the Round Table. He was always the best of us, the most pure in heart. He should have carried the Lance after me... but he rode off with his young friend Percival in search of the Grail, and we never saw either of them again. I tried to go back, of course. But I couldn't find the way. I haven't seen Elaine since I left the Grail Castle, and now my poor boy Galahad's dead, and probably Percival too." He gave her a stern look. "So now maybe you understand why your mother doesn't want you to go chasing after the Grail, Princess?"

"Does my mother know about Lady Elaine?" Rhianna demanded, clenching her fists.

Lancelot smiled. "There are no secrets between me and Guinevere."

Rhianna sighed. Then she had a sudden suspicion. "Do you know who Arianrhod's mother is?"

Sir Lancelot frowned. "Your maid's mother? No."

"But you know she came from the Grail Castle too, don't you? I found that out from the Crown, only she doesn't know who her father is… is it you? Is that why Arianrhod was left at Camelot as a baby?"

Lancelot guffawed. "I know I've got a reputation as a ladies' man, Princess, but you can't blame me for every waif who turns up at our gates! If the girl is mine, it's the first I know about it. Now then, get on up to your room and change into something pretty to please your mother. And remember – not a word about what happened at the Round Table after she left. She'll only get upset, you dragging up ghosts from the past."

He opened the door and held Excalibur out to her.

"You can't stop me going to look for the Grail," Rhianna told him, taking back her sword in relief. She strapped it around her waist and fingered the hilt thoughtfully. "If you were a *real* knight, you'd come with me to find your wife—"

Lancelot's blade glittered out of its scabbard and blocked her path. "You, my girl, are going the right way about getting locked in the dungeons like your maid did last year!" he growled.

Rhianna's heart thumped as Excalibur's jewel brightened in the gloom. "I won't let you do that to me," she said, ready to fight for her freedom if she had to.

Sweet Avalonian music, tinkling along the passage, distracted her. She saw Elphin on the steps, his harp balanced on one knee, watching them with his violet eyes. The anger left her, and she let her blade slip back into its scabbard.

Sir Lancelot sheathed his blade, too. "You've got guts, Princess, I'll give you that," he said. "Just wait for Sir Bors and the others to get back from the Tor before you ride off after the Grail, all right? Because I've had my fill of quests. She's all yours," he added as he brushed past Elphin. "Maybe you can talk some sense into her, because I can't seem to."

The champion knight marched off, muttering to himself.

"Are you all right, Rhia?" Elphin touched her bruised wrist in concern. "I heard shouting. Did Sir Lancelot hurt you?"

"Don't fuss," she said, pulling her sleeve down to cover the bruise. "It's nothing. I've had worse from Mordred and his bloodbeards."

"But Sir Lancelot's one of your father's knights! If you're having trouble with them, you should tell me. I might be able to help."

"Oh yes, put them all to sleep with your harp. Very useful." But she smiled at her friend. "I want them to help me look for the Grail, that's all. But now Sir Bors and Sir Bedivere are riding off to the Lonely Tor to investigate Gareth's death, and Sir Lancelot won't leave my mother's side. I'm sure he doesn't want me to complete my quest and bring King Arthur back."

Elphin smiled as well. "He's probably just trying to protect you."

"Maybe." She sighed. "But Sir Lancelot's actually been to the Grail Castle, and he still won't show me the way. Even Cai's riding off to the Lonely Tor with Sir Bors and the others...

You'll come with me, won't you Elphin?"

Her friend glanced back up the stairs, where there was a clatter of weapons and armour as the knights sorted out what to take on their trip to the Tor. Her stomach fluttered as she realised her friend was wearing his cloak. Merlin's spiral pathfinder glinted around his neck.

"Elphin?" she said.

"I have to go with them, Rhia," he said gently. "That's what I was coming to tell you. The Lonely Tor is the gateway to Avalon, and there might be some truth in your vision. I'm worried about my people."

"But Gareth didn't even drown at the Tor." She blinked at her friend in disbelief. "The Saxons said they found his body in the river."

"Possibly," Elphin said, his eyes serious. "But I still need to check the Tor's secure. You don't want to go to all the trouble of collecting the four Lights for your father, only to find the crystal caverns have been destroyed when we get back to Avalon, do you?"

Her stomach fluttered again. "Lord Avallach would never let anything happen to the crystal caverns! They're protected by magic – that's why Merlin took my father's body to Avalon in the first place."

Elphin nodded as he bagged his harp. "They always used to be protected. But Mordred used the Crown to open the gate of Annwn last year, and you have three of the Lights in one place now. The balance of power has changed. I'm not sure what'll happen if you find the Grail and take it through the mists to Avalon, but when all four Lights come together it's sure to cause some kind of magical disturbance."

"*When* I find the Grail," Rhianna corrected, trying to ignore the shiver his words had sent down her spine.

"All right, *when*." Her friend smiled. "Don't worry, we shouldn't be long. Then, of course I'll come with you to look for the fourth Light. I'll take Merlin with me and send him with a message if we need help. Just promise you won't try wearing the Crown of Dreams again until I get back."

"But—"

He gripped her arm with a six-fingered hand. His eyes deepened to purple. "Promise me, Rhia! Or I'll take that crown with me, too, even if it kills me like it killed Mordred."

Rhianna sighed. He was serious. She must have really scared him in the stables, earlier.

"I promise," she said.

3

Ship of Mist

Arthur's knights sought the isle of song,
Through storm and flood their road lay long.
While in the greenwood his queen did ride,
Gathering blossoms like a bride.

Rhianna watched from her tower window as her friends trotted out of the gates. Cai rode a new black mare with the Lance of Truth balanced on his stirrup like a proper knight. Sir Bors and Sir Bedivere led a party of older squires – Gareth's friends, on their first proper mission. Elphin and Evenstar, already a long way in front, misted through the trees, while the merlin flew ahead.

Cai glanced back up at the Damsel Tower and waved. Rhianna resisted a sudden urge to lean out of the window and order him back. She couldn't help thinking of last spring, when the knights had left her under guard in her room while they rode north to meet Mordred and got ambushed by bloodbeards on the road. This time, she had stayed of her own choice so she could look for the Grail. But that didn't make watching her friends leave any easier.

"Do you wish you'd gone with them, my lady?" Arianrhod asked, peering past her.

"No," Rhianna said, reaching for her Avalonian armour. "I've got more important things to do than find out how Gareth drowned.

Pack a picnic, Arianrhod! We'll ride up to the lake where I found Excalibur, and if it's not the lake Sir Galahad meant then we'll ask Lady Nimue if she knows the way to the Grail Castle – it's as good a place to start as any."

"Now?" her maid frowned. "But it's starting to rain, and aren't you supposed to be having lunch with your mother? It'll take us half a day to get up there, so we won't be back before dark…" Her voice trailed off at Rhianna's expression. "I'm sorry, Lady Rhia, of course I'll come with you if you need me, but what shall I tell the queen?"

Rhianna sighed. The last thing she needed was another argument with her mother. And her maid was right about the rain, which was blowing in from the marshes in dark sheets. The weather wouldn't stop her riding to the lake, of course – she'd ridden through worse on her quests for the first three Lights. But it would make the queen suspicious about their excuse of a picnic.

"Tomorrow, then," she said, reluctantly replacing the armour in her clothing chest and allowing her friend to help her into a dress instead. "The others won't be back from the Tor until tomorrow night at least. If we set out early, we'll still be back before them."

With the Grail of Stars, she thought hopefully.

Lunch with her mother was not quite as bad as she'd feared. Guinevere approved of the dress Arianrhod had picked out for her, and of the way Rhianna had let the knights and her friends ride out to the Tor without making a fuss. The queen seemed embarrassed about the slap she'd given her earlier, and obviously wanted to make up for it.

Rhianna stayed on her best behaviour. Towards the end of lunch, she lowered her gaze and asked if she and Arianrhod could take a picnic up to the lake the next day to exercise her horse.

The queen hesitated. "I don't know, darling," she said. "The villains who robbed that poor squire could still be at large."

"I've got Excalibur," Rhianna pointed out. "And we'll take some men with us, I promise. Whoever attacked Gareth probably fled when they saw the Saxons coming. Mordred's dead now, so he can't cause any trouble. Please, Mother? The knights don't think my vision meant anything, and it's been such a long winter."

"You're right about that, darling," Guinevere

said, gazing out of the window. "We've let Mordred and his bloodbeards terrorise us long enough. I might even come with you to gather some May blossom. We should be safe enough if we stay close to Camelot, and the castle needs cheering up a bit after the mess Mordred made while he was here. When Bors and Bedivere get back, I think we'll invite Chief Cynric and his Saxons to a feast to thank them for their help last year – we should show them how we celebrate spring at Camelot."

"We can easily bring some blossom back for you, Mother," Rhianna said sweetly. "You don't have to come with us – Arianrhod can gather it. I'm sure you're very busy here with Sir Lancelot."

Her mother gave her a sharp look. "Lancelot can come, too. I'll feel happier if he's looking after you." She pushed her plate aside and smiled. "I'm sorry I lost my temper with you in the meeting, darling. I think we were all a bit upset by that poor boy who drowned."

❧❧

Rhianna spent that evening trying to find out more about Sir Galahad and why he had died on his Grail Quest. But the other damsels giggled and said she could forget about the handsome knight, because he would never look at anyone except his friend Percival, and anyway, she'd make Elphin jealous. Rhianna went to bed in disgust.

The next day dawned wet, with rain that bounced off the roofs and made puddles in the yard. Not even Rhianna could pretend it was a good day for a picnic. She groomed Alba's white coat until it shone, and combed out the little mare's tail so many times that Alba complained she would have no hairs left by the time they got back to Avalon.

No word came from the knights who had ridden out to the Lonely Tor, which worried her slightly. But Sir Lancelot said they must have taken shelter to wait out the storm, and Rhianna didn't want to alarm the queen into cancelling their picnic, so she kept quiet about Elphin's promise to send Merlin back with a message if they needed help.

By the time the sun finally came out on the third day, she was as irritable as her horse. When the queen suggested they wait another day for the ground to dry out, she had to bite her lip to stop herself from starting another public argument with her mother.

"Alba needs to go out," she said as they stood in the puddle-filled yard, looking up at the sky. "Avalonian horses are highly strung. She'll kick down the stable, otherwise."

I cannot kick down the stable, Alba reminded her. *My hooves will mist through the wall.*

Rhianna giggled, and Sir Lancelot gave her a suspicious look. But the queen gave in. "Saddle my palfrey," she told the squires. "And find some sacks to hold the blossom."

The boys rushed to obey.

Rhianna saddled Cai's old mount, Sandy, for Arianrhod to ride. The pony seemed pleased someone had remembered him and blew into her hair.

"Just hold on to Sandy's mane," she told her friend. "He's got plenty of it. You'll be fine."

"I'd rather walk, my lady," Arianrhod said.

"Not through those puddles, you won't," Rhianna said. She mounted Alba and touched the bulge in the bottom of her pack where she'd hidden the Crown of Dreams. She didn't know if she would need it, but she felt uneasy leaving one of the Lights at Camelot unprotected.

Guinevere took ages settling herself side-saddle on a pretty golden mare with a creamy mane and tail. Finally, though, they were all mounted and clattering out through the gates.

Rhianna's spirits lifted as they rode. The sun shone warm on her face, and the rain had made everything smell fresh. Trees were just breaking into leaf. The meadows steamed around them as they crossed the bridge and turned up the road towards Nimue's lake. As the track stretched soft and green before them, Alba snatched at her bit and kicked up her heels.

I want to gallop!

Some of their escort's horses bucked. Sir Lancelot grabbed the queen's reins to steady her prancing palfrey. "Not today, my darling," Rhianna said, steadying the mare. "Or Arianrhod and my mother will fall off."

Alba snorted in disappointment. But she bent her neck obediently, and amused herself by crossing the puddles without getting her hooves wet.

They entered the wood, where the smell of wild garlic filled the air. White blossom lined their path, which the queen insisted upon stopping to gather at once. Arianrhod dismounted to help her tie the branches over Sandy's back, while Rhianna waited impatiently.

At last the queen was ready to move on, though they went even slower than before now that Arianrhod was leading Sandy with his burden of flowers. As they passed the battlefield where Mordred had killed King Arthur, everyone went quiet. Sir Lancelot whispered something to Guinevere, who shook her head.

Rhianna looked across the river with a shudder of memory. All the bodies had been buried, floods had washed the meadow clean, and wildflowers bloomed over the blood-soaked earth. But she still remembered the ghosts she had seen in this place when they first rode out of Avalon, and how scared she had been.

I do not like this place, Alba snorted.

Rhianna patted the mare's neck. "Don't worry, my darling. The Wild Hunt took all the ghosts away last winter. They won't be back."

The wood was more overgrown than she

remembered, and she wondered if they would find the secret path to the lake. Then a wind rippled the surface of the river and parted the branches, and she saw the familiar trail winding between the bushes.

"There it is!"

As she headed Alba up the overgrown path, a warning screech came from the trees ahead of them, and a small blue-grey falcon flew right under the mare's nose. Alba misted to avoid trampling the bird. Rhianna nearly fell off. The men drew their swords as the little falcon darted past them, spooking their horses too. Green mist curled along the trail in its wake.

"*Merlin...?*" Rhianna twisted in the saddle, her heart thumping. She fumbled Excalibur out of its scabbard so she could talk to the druid's spirit, if it was him.

But the merlin had banked sharply overhead, darted back and disappeared into the mist again. They heard faint shouts from the lake and the sound of splashing.

"Someone's up there," grunted Sir Lancelot. "Careful, Princess—"

Rhianna was already galloping after the merlin, sword in hand. The champion knight muttered a curse and came after her, but his big horse was slow through the wood and she arrived at the lake first.

Mist curled over its surface, and white lilies bloomed around the shore, just as they had when she'd dived into the depths to claim Excalibur from Lady Nimue. It had been winter then, but magic lingered in this place all year round. Rhianna could see no sign of the merlin. But something big creaked across the water, and a tall silvery mast glimmered in the mist. She halted Alba on the beach and stared at it, her neck prickling.

Just like her vision... except the ghostly ship was turning *away* from the shore, back into the enchanted mists.

She urged Alba on to the surface of the lake, in front of the ship. "Wait!" she called, her stomach churning as the big prow loomed over her. "I know it's been a while since you told us to meet you, but I'm here now! Don't go without me, please."

Hooves crashed through the wood behind her as the others caught up. She heard her mother's voice calling, "Rhianna darling, don't be so foolish! Lancelot says we should go back now..."

This ship has ghosts on board, Alba reported.

"I know it does, my darling," Rhianna said, steadying the mare. "Don't worry, they're friendly ghosts." She hoped so, anyway.

Excalibur shone brightly in her hand, lighting up the deck. The golden-haired Sir Galahad wrenched at the tiller to avoid her, while a lanky young ghost with dark hair clung to the rail, staring queasily at Rhianna and Alba as the ship slid past. It took her a moment to recognise the drowned squire, Gareth. A shiver went down her spine as she realised he must have been the boy lying on the deck in her vision.

"Sir Galahad!" she called. "You promised to take me to your mother's castle, remember?"

The ship slowed, and the ghostly knight eyed her sword. "Don't try to control me with your magic, Princess – I nearly ran you down!

I thought you would be alone. I cannot take my father Lancelot as well. He failed the test of the Grail."

"Sir Lancelot only came to look after the queen," Rhianna said quickly. "He's taking her back to Camelot now. I can come with you, can't I? I haven't failed the Grail test." She thought uneasily of Lady Nimue's final riddle about the fourth Light, that she had yet to answer correctly: *What does the Grail contain?* "I'll need my maid, too," she added.

Back on shore, Arianrhod had finally caught up and was staring, wide-eyed, at the ship. Sir Galahad frowned at the girl as she led her pony closer. "Isn't that Morgan Le Fay's maid?"

"Not any more," Rhianna said. "She's my friend now."

"I am forbidden to take anyone living who

is not on a Grail Quest," the ghostly knight insisted. "It's against the rules of this ship."

"Arianrhod's mother was a Grail maiden," Rhianna said, getting impatient with all the magical rules. "And she hasn't seen her since she was a baby, so she *is* on a Grail Quest... Sort of, anyway." She clutched Excalibur tighter and hardened her voice. "I'm King Arthur's daughter. I can't travel alone. If you won't take us, I'll follow you on Alba until you do."

"She will, too," muttered Gareth's ghost. "And that's a fairy horse she's riding, so you might as well let her come."

Sir Galahad frowned at the squire. He gave Alba a closer look and turned his ship back towards the shore. "Hurry up then, Princess. The way between worlds will not stay open for long."

As the big curved prow nudged the beach, the men closed protectively around their queen. Sir Lancelot scowled as a rope ladder swung over the side.

"Don't even think about it, Princess," he growled, trotting his stallion towards Rhianna. "Your mother will never forgive me if I let you go sailing off into the mist after a Grail that killed my son and half Arthur's knights too! Nobody returns alive after seeing that thing."

"I will return." Rhianna rode Alba around the prow to evade the knight. Excitement shivered through her. "Take my pack and get on board, Arianrhod," she whispered as she passed the maid. "I'm coming too, don't worry."

Arianrhod still looked scared. But she lifted Rhianna's pack containing the Crown of Dreams off Sandy's back, waded into the shallows and clambered awkwardly up the ladder. Sir Lancelot urged his horse into the water to stop the maid.

Rhianna gripped Excalibur tighter and concentrated, reaching for Sir Lancelot's spirit. She'd never tried to control her father's champion knight before, and her heart thumped.

"Sir Lancelot!" she ordered. "By this Sword that is linked to your knightly spirit, I command you! Take my mother back to Camelot, then ride to the Lonely Tor and find Cai and Elphin and the others. I'll meet you there. If I don't return with the Grail of Stars before midsummer, then you're to take the Lance of Truth back to Camelot and wait for me. I'll be back as soon as I can."

Excalibur's blade brightened, and the white

jewel on its hilt flashed at the sound of her voice.

Sir Lancelot spun his horse in a circle and glared at her. He did not seem to know which of them to come after first. Rhianna smiled and trotted Alba a bit further away from Arianrhod and the ship. Maybe this would be easier than she'd thought? Then the queen shouted, "Don't just stand there, Lancelot! My daughter's not sailing off on a ghost ship to God knows where! Stop them!"

Lancelot shook his head, as if waking from a daze. He urged his stallion deeper, trying to catch Arianrhod's wrist. But the horse, up to its belly now in the lake, refused to go near the ship with the two ghosts on deck. It reared and spun round, and Sir Lancelot – caught off balance – fell off over its tail with a loud splash.

Arianrhod giggled as the knight struggled to his feet, spluttering and spitting out the shining water.

Even though she felt bad about using the Sword of Light against her father's champion, Rhianna smiled too. "You can't stop us going," she called. "So don't try to follow us. Your horses can't gallop across water like Alba so you'll have to swim, and then you might drown like poor Gareth did."

"We'll see about that!" Lancelot struggled chest-deep through the water on foot, and made a final grab for the ladder. But it swung out of reach as Arianrhod reached the top and pulled the ladder up after her. The ship glided away from the shore, and Rhianna trotted Alba around the floundering knight to follow.

"*Rhianna!*" Queen Guinevere wailed.

"Rhianna darling, come back..." The men made a half-hearted attempt to give chase, but shook their heads when their horses refused to enter the water too.

Rhianna held Excalibur shining over her head, using its magic to stop Sir Lancelot from trying to swim after them, until the ship had reached deeper water. Then she sheathed her sword and galloped Alba after the ghostly vessel, her mare's enchanted horseshoes skimming across the surface of the lake. With the spray on her cheeks and her hair tugging loose from its braids, she laughed.

Her mother would worry, but that couldn't be helped. Looking for the Grail was more important than decorating Camelot with flowers.

DARK CAPTIVE

"M-my lord?" A timid finger poked Mordred's mortal hand. "There's a boat coming through the mist… you said to wake you if anyone came across from the mainland."

"I *said* not to touch me!" Mordred snatched his fist to his chest and glared at the woman who had woken him. It took him a moment to recognise Gareth's mother, who looked more skeletal than Uther's warriors since he'd drowned her son. She was breathing hard from her run up the hill to the chapel. He checked his hand, but she had not tried to remove the gauntlet – as if she'd dare.

He strode to the window and peered into the mist. His shadow-eyes were much sharper than his old mortal eyes, but even they could not see through the enchantments that surrounded the Tor. He saw his bloodbeards running along the beach with drawn weapons, followed by the screeching shadrake. The villagers watched silently from the doors of their huts, and the monks crossed themselves.

On the water, Mordred made out a blurred shape shining silver-bright. Green mist swirled around it, but he knew magic when he saw it.

Excitement stirred as a white horse emerged briefly from the mist and shook its mane. Its rider looked up at the Tor, something shining in its hand. "That's no boat, woman!

Don't you know a mist horse of Avalon when you see one?"

He had not expected his cousin so soon. But maybe she had given up on her doomed quest for the Grail of Stars, and was bringing the other three Lights to Avalon to see if they would work without the fourth? He was ready to give her the shock of her life.

Howling eagerly, Uther's ghosts chased the fairy horse back into the mist. Flashes of silver and green lit up the horizon, and faint shouts carried over the water. Mordred thought he saw a ship with billowing white sails and the fairy horse galloping after it, riderless. Then the stupid shadrake shrieked and flapped after them, and both ship and horse vanished in a flash of white light. After a pause, the dragon reappeared chasing

something small and dark that dived into
the sea.

His bloodbeards splashed into the shallows
with shouts of: "Get him!... Don't let him get
away!... Watch its claws!... Look out!"

Blinded by the flash, at first Mordred
could not see what was happening. Then his
captain emerged dragging something through
the water that splashed and struggled. He
squinted at it eagerly. Had they managed to
capture his cousin?

But the captive remained a blur of light and
shadow, and it looked much too small to be
human... the magic must have confused him.

He seized the woman's hair and dragged
her to the window.

"Look there!" he growled. "What do you
see?"

She blinked at the bloodbeard, who was now striding up the winding path to the chapel.

"Your c-captain, my lord," she said. "Carrying some kind of hawk."

"A hawk? Are you sure?"

Mordred pushed the woman aside. Now he could see it too – a bundle of bedraggled blue feathers hanging upside down in his bloodbeard's grip.

He laughed. "It's Merlin! Better a bird in the hand than a dragon in the mist, wouldn't you agree?"

Gareth's mother gave him another frightened look.

"Well, don't just stand there, woman! Bring me that candelabra from the altar – our guest will need a perch when he arrives.

Then get back down to the beach and tell my men to keep a good lookout out for that ship. We don't want any nasty surprises."

He waited until his bloodbeard captain had leashed the soggy merlin to the candelabra. Then he lit the candles to form a cage of fire, and watched the bird curiously. Was the druid's spirit still trapped inside its little body?

The merlin flapped upside down, spraying water and making the flames hiss. Mordred let it tire itself out and reached over the nearest candle with his shadow-hand. He lifted the exhausted bird back on to the candelabra, where it glared at him, beak open and wings spread.

"Such a fragile body," Mordred said. "I'm surprised you're still using it, druid. The mist magic too much for you these days, eh? That's the trouble when you grow old and slow. You start to make mistakes. Don't worry, though, we'll soon have you dried out."

The merlin beat its wings in anger. Sparks flew as its feathers brushed the candle flames.

Mordred laughed. "Be careful, druid. Fire hurts, and I should know. I assume you're here because your knights found the squire's body? So sad, a young boy drowning like that, but these marshes are dangerous places for the unwary."

The merlin screeched and stabbed his shadow-hand with its beak.

Mordred laughed and wriggled his fingers. "Can't harm *this* body, druid," he said.

The merlin screeched again.

"What was that?" Mordred leaned closer,

pretending to listen. "Oh yes, I forgot – I can't hear what you're saying unless I'm holding one of the Lights. But my cousin has the Sword, her useless squire has the Lance, the Crown is at Camelot, and the Grail is still lost. How annoying! You'll just have to wait until she brings Excalibur here before you can talk to me. I assume that was her riding her fairy horse out in the mist with you so she shouldn't be long now. Then you can tell me how to take my men through the mists to Avalon. I've some unfinished business with my dear Uncle Arthur."

The merlin stuck its head under its wing.

Behind him, his captain cleared his throat. Mordred frowned. He had forgotten the bloodbeard was still there. "What?" he said.

"Er, sorry to interrupt, master… but I think

the fairy horse was being ridden by the Avalonian boy."

Mordred gave him a frustrated look. "What about that ship I saw?"

"We didn't see anybody else, master."

Mordred grabbed the merlin's tail. "If this is some kind of trick…" But he'd forgotten to use his shadow-hand. The merlin's sharp beak stabbed his gauntlet, and green pus oozed out as its talons sank into his wrist. He shook the bird off and hugged his throbbing hand to his chest.

"You'll be sorry you did that!" he yelled. "I don't need to keep you alive if the fairy prince is here with your druid charm – he can show us the way to Avalon. You'll be much more use as lunch."

But as he gripped the bird's neck, the

bloodbeard cleared his throat again. Mordred scowled. "What *now*?" he snapped.

"Er, what if the fairy drowned, master? I've heard they don't swim too well..."

Mordred unclenched his fist and his temper cooled.

He scowled at the bedraggled bird. "You've had a lucky escape, druid." Ignoring the merlin's scolding, he turned his scowl on the bloodbeard. "What are you still doing here? Go find me the rider of that fairy horse... bring whoever it is to me, dead or alive. And while you're at it, find a hood for this hawk. That'll keep it quiet until I know if we need its help. Quickly, man – *run*!"

The bloodbeard ran.

◀◗ 4 ◖▶

Missing Elphin

Across the lake there came a sail
Bringing the knight who found the Grail,
When a riderless horse did reappear
To raise Rhianna's darkest fear.

At first, the triumph of escaping Sir Lancelot and her mother kept the grin on Rhianna's face. Then she remembered the way the merlin had vanished into the mist and sobered. If the ship was travelling between worlds, she didn't want to lose sight of it as well.

She rode Alba alongside the ship. Gareth's ghost took one look at her fairy horse trotting on the water, groaned and went below. Arianrhod leaned over to speak to her, clutching the wooden rail with white knuckles.

"Where are we going, my lady?" she whispered.

"To the Grail Castle, of course, to find your mother and collect the Grail of Stars." Rhianna glanced at Sir Galahad half expecting the golden-haired young knight to fade from sight now that she had sheathed Excalibur. She only hoped the ship wouldn't vanish with him. But obviously the magical rules worked differently out here. Lancelot's son stood at the tiller, watching her from his pale eyes.

"Did you see a merlin, earlier?" she called. "It flew off into the mist when you arrived."

Galahad shook his head. "No, Princess. But I expect it'll find its way back to Camelot eventually. Hawks usually do if they get lost hunting."

She wondered if she should tell him about Merlin's spirit being inside the falcon's body, and admit her friends had taken him to the Lonely Tor in case they needed to call for help. But the merlin they had seen in the wood might have been an ordinary wild bird, and she didn't want to distract Galahad from their quest.

"How far is it to the Grail Castle?" she asked.

Sir Galahad smiled. "Nobody knows, Princess. The way changes all the time."

She scowled. Now he sounded like Merlin. "How long will it take to get there, then?"

"It depends on the mists." The knight frowned at a dark patch behind them. "We weren't alone when they opened just now. I think something's following us. It might be safer if you came aboard, Princess."

"I prefer to ride," Rhianna said, resting her hand on Excalibur's hilt. The white jewel shone brightly, its light spilling between her fingers. "Don't worry. Alba's a mist horse so she can follow anywhere your ship can go. And I carry the Sword of Light so I can fight if need be."

Sir Galahad frowned at her. "That's not exactly what I meant. The Grail Castle is well defended. When we arrive, this ship will be allowed to land, but if the guardians see you riding a fairy horse they're likely to react badly. The Wild Hunt is not welcome at the Grail Castle. We have souls to protect."

"The souls of the knights killed by the Grail, you mean?" Rhianna said.

"Yes." Galahad said. "It might kill you, too. Aren't you scared, Princess?"

"No." Rhianna wondered for the first time what would happen if she failed to win the Grail. "If I die on my quest the Wild Hunt will take my soul back to Avalon."

"Those who have seen the Grail of Stars don't belong anywhere the fairy lord can take them," Galahad said, drawing himself up and suddenly looking very like a younger version of Sir Lancelot. His eyes gleamed, and his hand moved to the ghostly blade at his side. "If Avallach comes for my soul, I will fight him every step of the way."

Rhianna shivered. "I'm sure Lord Avallach won't take it if you don't want him to, Sir Galahad," she said. "I'll ask him not to."

Galahad threw back his head and laughed.

"And why do you think the fairy lord will listen to *you*, Rhianna Pendragon?"

"Because he looked after me when I was little, so he's practically my father, that's why." She glanced across the deck, half expecting her father's ghost to appear and remind her she was human. But Arianrhod stood alone at the rail, her fingers twisting nervously into her skirt as she listened to their conversation. "He'll listen to his son, Elphin, if he doesn't listen to me," she added. "Prince Elphin's waiting for us on the Lonely Tor."

Evenstar's rider not on lonely hill, Alba said, flattening her ears.

A sudden wind tugged at the mare's mane, and a pale shadow rippled towards them across the water. Rhianna heard faint splashing like someone rowing very fast.

Arianrhod gasped. "It's another ghost, my lady!"

Rhianna drew Excalibur and the sword's blade gleamed as she looked for an enemy to fight. The splashing drew closer, but she still couldn't see anything.

Then, in a blur of silver, a horse appeared right in front of them. She only just stayed in the saddle as her mare misted to avoid a crash. Alba neighed a welcome, and Rhianna knew how the other horse had got so close without them seeing it coming – it had misted, too.

"It's Evenstar!" She laughed in relief. When the mists opened, her friend must have taken a shortcut back from the Tor using the spiral path, like they had done between stone circles on their quest for the Lance of Truth.

"*Faha'ruh*, Elphin!" she said, turning her

mare. "What were you trying to do, scare us to…"

The words died in her throat as Evenstar trotted up to Alba, arched his neck and blew into the mare's nostrils. His reins were tangled around his knees, and his beautiful silver coat dripped with green slime.

Rhianna stared at his empty saddle in confusion. She felt a bit sick. But realising she was upsetting both mist horses, she pulled herself together. "What have you done with Elphin, you silly horse?" she said. "Ask Evenstar what happened, Alba."

The two mist horses touched nostrils, and Alba snorted.

He say a dragon chase him, the mare reported. *He say his rider fall off in the water. He was frightened and get lost in mist. I am frightened, too.*

Rhianna stroked the mare's trembling neck and frowned into the mist. But she could see no sign of a dragon chasing Evenstar. "There's no need to be, my darling," she said. "It's gone now, whatever it was."

"What did Evenstar say?" Arianrhod asked.

"He says Elphin fell off. Evenstar must have panicked and got trapped on the wrong side when the mists closed." She tried to sound cheerful for her maid's sake. But her stomach refused to settle. She kept imagining her friend falling into the water, and his dark curls disappearing beneath the surface.

Elphin can't swim, she remembered, feeling sick again.

Sir Galahad looked at Evenstar and nodded gravely. "I've heard fairy horses from the enchanted isle can be tricky to ride. At least that explains what's been following us. Maybe we can continue our voyage now."

Rhianna gave the knight a distracted look. "No, we've got to find Elphin first. Take us to the Lonely Tor!"

But Sir Galahad shook his head. "I'm sorry, Princess, I can't do that. This ship does not sail lightly in the world of men, and if your fairy prince fell off in the enchanted mists he might be anywhere. I'm afraid you need to make a choice. Your friend or the Grail… which is it to be?"

Rhianna gazed across the water, undecided. She could see no sign of life, just the endless mist over a shining white sea, rather like her visions whenever she used the Crown of Dreams to look for the Grail. But she couldn't abandon her friend. She gathered up Alba's reins.

Arianrhod grasped the rail. "Lady Rhia!" she gasped. "Don't leave me on this ship, please! Elphin's got Merlin's spiral pathfinder, remember. He'll be able to find us easier than we'll find him."

Rhianna looked at the maid's terrified face and knew her friend was right. Elphin would survive without his horse for a bit. He had his magic harp, too, and he was of the immortal Avalonian race so he couldn't drown like Gareth had done. Whatever had happened when the mists opened, he would be all right until they got back to the land of men. Whereas if she rode off into the mists looking for him, she might lose the ship and her only chance of finding the fourth Light.

"I won't leave you, silly," she said. "You're the only Grail maiden I know. I need you to help me take the Grail of Stars to Avalon, once we find it."

Arianrhod relaxed slightly. "You'll need the Lance of Truth as well, won't you? So we'll have to find Cai, too."

Rhianna sighed. "Cai too," she promised. "Will you help us look for our friends on the way back, Sir Galahad? They went to the Lonely Tor together, so Elphin might still be with Cai."

"Sir Kai's boy?" Galahad shook his head. "You'll be better off without that clumsy squire. Couldn't even ride, as I remember."

"Well, he can ride now, *and* he's fought dragons," Rhianna said, her blood rising. "Which is more than you ever have, I bet!"

Galahad regarded her in amusement. "It seems you know as much about me as I know about you and your friends, Princess. All right, if you survive the test of the Grail I promise to bring you back as far as the Lonely Tor. Are you coming aboard now? It'll be dark soon, and when the night wind picks up we'll go faster. Not many people can follow this ship in the dark, not even in their dreams."

Arianrhod peered nervously past the ghost. "Please come aboard, Rhia," she said. "You have to eat something. You haven't had a bite since breakfast."

Rhianna pulled a face. Food was the last thing on her mind. But Sir Galahad's words had given her an idea how she might find out what had happened to Elphin.

She patted Alba's neck. "Stay with Evenstar," she whispered to the mare. "I need to wear my crown for a bit, and I can't ride you as well."

She made sure her shield was secure. Then she stood in the saddle and vaulted lightly over the rail to join Arianrhod aboard the Grail ship.

꧁❀꧂

Considering it had been built for ghosts, the ship carried plenty of supplies. They found a sack of juicy apples, another of biscuits, and a barrel of something fizzy. While Arianrhod unpacked the picnic they had brought from Camelot, Gareth's ghost reappeared and crouched beside them. He tried to pick up a honey cake and pulled a face when his fingers passed through it.

"Leave that alone!" Arianrhod said, shifting away from the ghost. "You're dead now so you can't eat it, anyway."

Gareth scowled at her. "I'm not hungry. I have to talk to Princess Rhianna."

"She's too tired," Arianrhod said.

But Rhianna looked curiously at the squire. "Do you remember how you died, Gareth?" she asked gently. "The Saxons said they found your body in the river."

The ghost scowled. "That makes sense, I suppose. Last thing I remember is Mordred's bloodbeards shoving my head underwater. Then next thing I know, I'm on this weird ship with Sir Galahad sailing through the mist."

"So it was bloodbeards!" Arianrhod said. "Sir Bors thought it was. Did they attack you on your way home?"

But Gareth shook his head impatiently. "I never got a chance to start for home. They attacked my family's village." He glanced across the shadowy deck and lowered his voice. "I saw Mordred over on the Tor," he whispered. "He had two hands."

"That's impossible," Rhianna said, her stomach fluttering as she remembered her vision. "You must have seen his ghost, that's all. We burned his body last year. You were there."

Gareth grimaced. "I know what I saw. There's magic at work in these mists, and it's not your fairy friend working it."

"What do you mean?" Rhianna demanded. "Do you know what's happened to Elphin, because if you do…" Her hand dropped to Excalibur's hilt.

"Steady!" Gareth raised his hands with a nervous laugh. "I can't be killed twice, you know. I haven't seen your fairy friend, but if he's gone across to the Tor then he'd better watch out for dark magic, that's all I'm saying."

"We're going there right after we find the Grail," Rhianna said. "So we'll soon find out if you're telling the truth or not."

Gareth shrugged. "I don't care if you don't believe me – the dark knight can't hurt me now. Pass me a drink, I want to try something."

Arianrhod held a cup for him. The squire slurped it down, grinned at them and belched loudly. The maid shuddered as the fizz fountained from Gareth's ghostly body.

Sir Galahad watched them with a strange look in his eye. Rhianna wondered if he missed the taste and offered him her cup, suddenly not thirsty any more. The ghost shook his head.

"Be careful what you drink when we reach the Grail Castle, Princess," was all he said.

Night fell, and water hissed under the

hull as they picked up speed. The ship glided smoothly through the mist, its sails glowing eerily blue. Alba and Evenstar trotted steadily behind it, too weary now to jump at shadows. Even more worried about Elphin after Gareth's tale of bloodbeards on the Tor, Rhianna tossed some apples into the water for them. Alba picked one up without breaking stride and crunched happily.

Nearly as sweet as Avalon apples! the mare said in surprise.

"Don't get left behind," Rhianna warned the two horses. "I'm going to wear my crown now. If Evenstar hears Elphin, wake me up at once."

I will listen for Elphin too, Alba said.

"Good girl."

Arianrhod was already curled up on the

deck, using her pack as a pillow. Sir Galahad reclined at the stern, steering with one ghostly foot on the tiller. Gareth was attempting to climb the mast, giggling when he fell back down. Rhianna frowned at the squire. Had he really seen Mordred's ghost on the Tor, or was he just trying to scare them?

She lay down on the deck next to her maid. Trying not to think of the promise she'd made Elphin, she slid the Crown of Dreams out of her pack.

Its jewels glittered in the dark, and she peered anxiously across the deck. But Sir Galahad was still watching Gareth's antics, and Arianrhod had gone to sleep. Rhianna laid Excalibur at her side. She took a deep breath and slipped the Crown of Dreams on to her head, pulling the cloak over it to hide the magic.

She lay listening to the hiss of water under the hull, and the snorts of the mist horses as they crunched the final few apples. She kept thinking of Evenstar's empty saddle and the little horse's claim that a dragon had chased him.

"Show me," she whispered.

But try as she might, the Crown remained cool. She couldn't even make it show her mist and water this time, though plenty of both swirled around them.

"*It's not your fault, daughter,*" a voice whispered in her ear. "*There is strong magic working against you. But I'm glad you chose to continue your quest.*"

She held her breath in sudden hope. King Arthur's ghost knelt beside her, his eyes very blue as they reflected the glow from the sails.

"Father!" she said. "Are you ready to return to your body now?"

"*Not quite yet,*" said the ghost. "*I don't want Galahad to see me. I'm not supposed to be on this ship, but you'll need your friends when you get to the Grail Castle. Listen.*"

At first Rhianna could hear nothing but the flap of sails as the wind changed. Then she heard music playing faintly in the night... the tinkle of a harp.

❄

"Rhia! My lady! Lady Rhia, wake up!"

Arianrhod was shaking her. The maid sounded excited. Rhianna sat up with a start. The Crown of Dreams rolled off her head, its jewels glittering in a luminous dawn.

"I thought you'd left that crown at Camelot,"

Arianrhod said, picking it up before it could fall into the sea.

It took Rhianna a moment to remember where she was. Then she saw the white sails of the ghost ship flapping above her. She looked round quickly for her father's ghost. It had gone, though – just a dream, after all. Her head throbbed from wearing the third Light.

"Why did you wake me?" she said. "I was trying to find out what happened to the others."

Arianrhod's face lit up. "It's Elphin's harp!" she said. "We've found them, Lady Rhia!"

Rhianna's heart quickened when she realised she could still hear the faint sound of a harp. But the music had no magic in it. "That's not Elphin playing," she said, frowning. "And it's out of tune, can't you hear?"

Arianrhod listened a moment, one hand

pressed to her scarred cheek. "It still sounds like his harp, though…"

Sir Galahad had heard the harp as well. He raised a ghostly eyebrow at Rhianna. "I suppose this is your doing, Princess. This ship never normally passes within sight or sound of shore, unless it's on Grail business. First a drowned squire, then a fairy horse, and now a ghostly harpist. Whatever next?"

"Mordred and his bloodbeards, maybe?" Gareth said, rippling into view again.

Rhianna scowled at the squire.

"We need to land," she said, getting to her feet and strapping Excalibur back around her waist. She rested a hand on the sword's hilt. "*Now.*"

Galahad sighed. "I knew you would be trouble the first time I saw you – a damsel carrying the Sword of Light! I thought I'd explained? Only the dead and those on a Grail Quest can come aboard this ship."

Rhianna drew Excalibur and sprang across the deck. She set the shining blade to Galahad's throat. "Land!" she commanded. "That's an order, sir knight."

Arianrhod sucked in her breath. She clutched Rhianna's pack with the Crown now safely inside, and stared from one ghost to the other.

Galahad smiled. "I'm already dead, Princess. Your blade can't command me."

"But *this* can," Rhianna said, concentrating on Excalibur's white jewel. After her practice commanding Sir Lancelot's spirit earlier, it was easier to control the magic this time.

Galahad stiffened and his hand jerked the

tiller over. The sails flapped as the ship turned towards the music on the shore. Arianrhod ducked as the boom swung across, nearly knocking her into the sea. Gareth grinned as it passed harmlessly through his ghostly body.

Galahad glared at Rhianna. "You'll have us over, you crazy girl! All right, you win. We'll go and see who is playing that harp so badly out there in the mist. But I'm not breaking the rules for you, King Arthur's daughter or no. I'm forbidden to take just anyone to the Grail Castle."

Rhianna nodded. But she kept Excalibur unsheathed as a grey line of beach showed ahead, wary of what they might find.

Their prow crunched on pebbles. Damp figures curled in their cloaks around a smouldering fire. A smaller figure, sitting on a rock at the edge of the shore, cradled the harp they had heard. He was plucking its strings between muffled sobs, and every so often a broken one twanged.

"It's Cai!" she said. Her heart gave a thud of relief, mixed with worry.

Further along the beach, Sir Bors and Sir Bedivere were pointing into the mist and arguing. Their horses, tethered under the trees, noticed the ship first. Sir Bors' stallion whinnied. Alba whinnied back. Evenstar gave a hopeful snort.

Startled, the two knights spun round. They drew their swords and came running back along the beach, shouting a warning to the others. The sleeping squires scrambled to their feet and groped for their weapons. They stared in confusion at the two riderless mist horses as they cantered out of the mist on to dry land.

Cai dropped the harp and ran to grab Alba's reins. "What have you done with Damsel Rhianna?" he shouted at the mare. "What were you doing galloping about out there with Evenstar? Where's Elphin?"

Rhianna couldn't help a smile. None of them had noticed the enchanted ship yet. "I'm up here, Cai!" she called, vaulting over the rail with Excalibur to land lightly beside him. "More to the point, what are you doing with Elphin's harp? Were you with him when he fell off? Is he all right?"

Cai sucked in his breath and blinked at her in surprise. "Damsel Rhianna! Where did you spring from?" He stared up at the curving prow of the ship, saw Arianrhod leaning over the rail with Gareth's ghost beside her, and blinked again. The other squires were staring up at the ship, too. One of them poked the glittering prow with a stick to see if it was real.

"I wouldn't do that unless you want to lose your fingers, boy!" Sir Galahad called down. The boy leaped back in alarm as he noticed the ghostly knight.

Sir Bors and Sir Bedivere arrived out of breath and stared at the ghosts, too.

"Gareth...?" Sir Bedivere said, his face breaking into a smile. "Is that really you up there, lad?"

"He's just a ghost," Rhianna said impatiently. "He drowned, remember. What happened to Elphin? Where did you lose him?"

Cai picked up the harp and gave her a stricken look. "He's gone, Damsel Rhianna. As soon as we got here, he galloped off across the water with your merlin and vanished into the mist. We tried to stop him but he was worried about his family, and our horses couldn't follow Evenstar across the water. Then the mist turned green with all these flashing lights, like when Merlin does magic, and now we can't find the Lonely Tor either! We made camp here to wait for him, but he never came back. I found his harp washed up on the beach last night..." He held it out to her. "A string's broken," he whispered.

Rhianna's blood turned cold as he spoke. Evenstar sniffed the harp sadly.

He say the music not work any more, Alba reported.

She took the harp from Cai, pushed Evenstar's nose away and touched the broken string. It twanged mournfully across the water.

"I'm sorry, Damsel Rhianna," Sir Bors said gruffly, frowning at Evenstar's empty saddle. "When the fairy lad opened the spiral path, we think some magic stopped him from getting back again. He's probably already in Avalon. I expect that's why the Lonely Tor disappeared."

"Yes, that must be it," Sir Bedivere said with forced cheerfulness. "I'm sure Elphin's just fine, Damsel Rhianna. Merlin's probably with him, wherever they are."

Rhianna shook her head. She thought of how Morgan Le Fay had ambushed them on this same stretch of water when she and Elphin had ridden out of Avalon at the start of her quest. "Gareth says the bloodbeards who drowned him attacked the Lonely Tor," she admitted. "He claims he saw Mordred's ghost over there, too."

"I know what I saw," Gareth said.

Everyone avoided looking at Rhianna. The knights glanced at each other, grave-faced. Gareth's friends shuffled their feet in the pebbles.

"So what do we do now?" Cai said.

Sir Bors looked at the ship. "Galahad can take us all over to the Tor, of course. It must be out there somewhere. A dirty great hill like that don't just disappear into thin air! Cai, go fetch your magic lance – if Damsel Rhianna's right, we might need it when we get over there. Keep your swords handy, boys. I don't like the look of them green mists."

Now Sir Bors was acting as if he commanded the ship. Although desperately worried about her friend, Rhianna shook her head again. If Mordred's ghost *was* on the Tor working some dark magic, she knew they couldn't risk going over there until she had found the Grail, no matter what trouble Elphin might be in.

She took a deep breath, thinking of her father. "We can't go looking for the Tor now," she said. "We're on our way to find the Grail of Stars."

"We can look for that thing after we've sorted out those bloodbeards who drowned Gareth," Sir Bors said firmly. "The queen ordered us to look into his death, and a knight must complete his duty."

Gareth looked smug. His friends nodded.

"That's *your* duty," Rhianna pointed out, resting her hand on Excalibur's hilt. "Not mine."

"Now be reasonable, Rhianna," Sir Bedivere

said. "Don't you want to find out what happened to your fairy friend?"

"Of course I do!" she said, her heart twisting. "But I need the Grail to wake my father. When we've got all four Lights, we'll be able to help those on the Tor as well as find Elphin more easily."

They would have to find Elphin eventually, because without the spiral pathfinder he wore, none of them could get back to Avalon. She just wished she could be in two places at once.

The knights began to argue about the power of the Lights, and whether Merlin would be of any help to the monks in his falcon body. But Sir Galahad interrupted them. "This ship sails on Grail duty," he reminded them. "I am forbidden to take anyone on board who is not on a Grail Quest."

Sir Bors scowled at him. "I've already seen your precious castle, don't forget. I went there with your father, Lancelot, before you were even born."

Galahad nodded. "Yes, I know, and you're welcome to escort the princess if you wish. I'm permitted to take her maid, too. But not you, Bedivere, I'm afraid. And none of your squires, except the dead lad. Ghosts are always welcome on this ship."

"What about me?" Cai said, running up with the Lance of Truth to join them. "I'm the Pendragon's champion now. I've got to stay with Damsel Rhianna in case she needs me to fight a duel for her."

One of Gareth's friends grinned. "You heard Sir Galahad. That ship takes nobody who's not good enough. Seems you got to stay and help us look after the horses, *Sir* Cai."

Cai swung his lance at the squires, who closed around him in a threatening manner.

Rhianna shoved the boys apart. She gripped Excalibur's hilt and concentrated on Sir Galahad's spirit. "Cai comes with us," she said firmly. "If he's good enough to carry the Lance of Truth, he's good enough to sail on your ship."

The ghostly knight looked closer at Cai's lance, which glittered in the mist like Excalibur's blade. "That's the lance my father stole from the Grail Castle!" he exclaimed.

"Lancelot didn't steal it," Sir Bors muttered. "He was given it by one of the damsels."

"By Lady Elaine?" said a small voice, and they all looked up in surprise. Rhianna had almost forgotten Arianrhod, who leaned over the rail beside Gareth's ghost, listening eagerly.

"How does the maid know about Elaine?" Sir Bors grumbled. "I thought Lancelot kept that part of his life a secret."

"Never mind," Rhianna said. "Cai comes with us, all right? Get on board, Cai. I'm going to ride Alba for a bit."

The boy passed the Lance of Truth up to Arianrhod, who lowered the rope ladder for him. Cai scrambled up, while Sir Bors splashed into the water and quickly grasped the end before Arianrhod could pull the ladder back again. "Take the other squires and find some boats," he called over his shoulder to Sir Bedivere. "We'll meet you on the Tor. See if you can't find that fool Lancelot on your way. I'm goin' to have something to say to him when I next see him… letting Damsel Rhianna and her maid sail off into the mist on *this* ship! What was he thinking?"

"I don't think Father had much choice, Bors," Sir Galahad said, looking at Rhianna in amusement. "She carries King Arthur's sword, and it seems she knows how to use it."

Sir Bors hauled himself aboard and scowled over the stern at Rhianna and Alba. "When you get back on this ship, young lady, you and I are going to have a serious talk."

Rhianna pretended not to hear. She slowed Alba to wait for Evenstar, who was trotting up and down the beach with his nose to the ground, trying to pick up his rider's scent. When she called him, the little horse galloped across the water and let her strap Elphin's harp to his saddle.

"Look after this harp for Prince Elphin,"

she told the worried horse, giving him a pat. "We'll rescue your rider as soon as I've found the last magic Light."

He say he will bite anyone who tries to steal it, Alba said, shaking her mane. *Why is the big knight angry with us?*

Rhianna watched Sir Bors shooing away Gareth's ghost. "He's not angry. He just doesn't understand magic."

As the mists closed around them once more, a shiver went down her spine. What did she really know about magic, despite having grown up in Avalon? Using the Sword of Light to control the knights' spirits had left her trembling, and she couldn't use the Crown of Dreams properly, not even to find her friend. Without Elphin at her side, with his violet eyes and his calming songs, she felt very alone.

"Elphin," she whispered. "Hold on, wherever you are. I'll be back to help you as soon as I can."

5

Grail Castle

A ghost ship sailed from mortal shore
Through mist and stars of ancient lore
To fish king's castle cloaked by night
Where maidens guard the greatest Light.

Rhianna knew she would have to face her friends eventually, but she put it off as long as possible. The moon had turned the mists to silver by the time she told Alba to trot alongside the ship so she could climb over the rail.

Sir Bors had lit torches on board so that the ship trailed fire through the night. He was holding a muttered conversation with Galahad at the tiller. Cai sat with Arianrhod near the mast. The maid had taken the Crown of Dreams out of her pack to polish its jewels, while Cai rested the Lance across his knees and glowered at Gareth's ghost whenever the dead squire tried to touch it. But as soon as they saw Alba at the rail, they both dropped their Lights and rushed over to help Rhianna aboard.

"Sir Bors isn't very pleased with you, Lady Rhia," Arianrhod warned, glancing at the big knight.

"He's probably calmed down by now," Cai said. "He's been talking to Sir Lancelot's son for ages. You wouldn't believe the adventures Sir Galahad had before he died! He's so young, too… I hope I have an exciting life like him."

Rhianna frowned. "Haven't you had enough adventures with me, looking for the four Lights? Or do you want to die on a quest, like Galahad did?"

Cai flushed. "I didn't mean that."

Sir Bors had spotted Rhianna. He came striding across the deck. She stiffened and her hand crept towards Excalibur.

But the big knight opened his arms to give her one of his crushing hugs. "If you thought you could sneak off with your maid to look for the Grail without me and Cai, Damsel Rhianna, you can think again. You don't get rid of us that easily."

"I would have taken you with me in the first place, if you hadn't gone riding off to the Lonely Tor with Elphin," she said, still angry with the knight for letting her friend ride into the mists alone.

Sir Bors grunted. "Well I'm here now, and I know my way around the Grail Castle so don't leave me behind again, right?" He held her at arm's length and looked her up and down. "I'm sorry I let the fairy lad ride off like he did, but I thought he'd be all right with his magic horse and Merlin. Bedivere and the others will find him, don't worry. I'm more worried about *us* getting back, to be honest. Not many who see the Grail return alive."

"We'll get back," Rhianna said, trying not to think of what might happen to Elphin if they didn't return. "I found the other three Lights, didn't I? And that was when I had to fight Mordred, his witch-mother and the shadrake for them! If Mordred's bloodbeards are over on the Tor like Gareth claims, at least we know they won't be waiting for us at the Grail Castle – even Mordred's ghost can't be in two places at once." She hoped not, anyway.

"Maybe not, but where we're going has its own dangers." Sir Bors glanced at Galahad's ghost and lowered his voice. "Let's assume you manage to get hold of this Grail that's killed Lancelot's son and just about everyone else who's ever laid eyes on it, and we find your fairy friend and get the through the mists to Avalon, *and* Merlin's right about Arthur waking up to finish off the bloodbeards and lead us all again... what are you going to do with the Lights afterwards, when your father is back on the throne of Camelot?"

Rhianna frowned. She hadn't really thought

much about it beyond giving Excalibur back to her father.

"We're going to keep them, of course!" Cai said, gripping the Lance of Truth. "So sneaky traitors like Mordred can't never kill the king again!"

As he spoke, the mists around them chilled and dimmed. The ghosts faded from view, and Rhianna thought she saw her father watching them from the shadows behind the mast.

"Keep your voice down, Cai," the big knight muttered, glancing out to sea. "I don't suppose I can talk you out of tryin' for the Grail now you've come this far. Just take care in the Grail Castle, both of you. I've been there, and they don't see things quite the same way men do."

"It's all right, Sir Bors," Rhianna said, keeping an eye on her father's ghost. "I've lived with Elphin's people in Avalon, and they don't see things the way men do, either."

When the big knight had gone, she quickly checked the deck, but King Arthur had vanished again. She settled back against the mast with a sigh and hugged her knees. The sails glowed blue again, and the mist flickered with coloured lights. Strong magic surrounded them – she knew that much from having taken the spiral path with Merlin. They must be far from the world of men now.

She dozed off thinking of Elphin and dreamed of racing their mist horses through Avalon's golden wood.

❈

A touch on her shoulder woke her. "Damsel Rhianna?" Cai said in a funny voice, his face glowing with coloured lights. "I think we're here."

She leaped to her feet and rubbed the sleep from her eyes. Ahead of them, a castle of stars floated out of the mist. Lights blazed from every window and spire, flickering gold and green in the night. When she looked more closely, she saw the castle actually stood on a tall rock, and the sea reflected the lights so that another magical castle appeared upside down, glittering in the dark water beneath.

"It's so beautiful!" Arianrhod breathed, her eyes full of stars.

Rhianna's heart pounded with excitement, and she pushed her worry for Elphin firmly to the back of her mind. The final stage of her quest! She mustn't make a mess of things now.

Everyone came up on deck to stare at the

enchanted castle as the ship drew into the harbour. They glided up against a quay, where strings of lanterns hung from posts carved to look like fish.

Grey-cloaked figures ran on silent feet to meet them. They pushed a plank across to the ship and formed two lines, bright eyes watching from under the grey hoods. Rhianna noted bows slung over their backs and full quivers strapped to their narrow waists. Her neck prickled.

Remembering Sir Galahad's warning, she looked anxiously for her mist horse. Alba and Evenstar were trotting up and down outside the harbour wall, nervous of the upside down castle rippling in the water under their hooves. "Hide!" she told Alba. "Find a quiet beach and wait for us. I've got to go into the castle now. I'll be back as soon as I can."

The two horses cantered off, flicking their tails.

Rhianna straightened her shoulders and took a deep breath. She waited until Arianrhod had packed away the Crown of Dreams, and Cai had picked up the Lance of Truth. Then she rested a hand on Excalibur, raised her chin and strode across the plank after Sir Galahad. Sir Bors hurried after them with Gareth's ghost treading on his heels.

Galahad led them to a pair of huge gates decorated with shells, where an old man who reminded Rhianna of Merlin stood waiting for them. He had blue eyes and long silver hair plaited with seaweed. He wore a flowing cloak embroidered with tiny glittering fish that rippled like the sea as he moved.

Galahad went down on one ghostly knee

and said, "I bring visitors from the land of men, Your Majesty. What is your command?"

The king frowned at them. "My guardians also reported seeing two horses from the fairy isle. Avalonians are not welcome here."

"We saw no one from the fairy isle on our way here, sire." Galahad glanced at Rhianna, who bit her lip at this reminder of her missing friend.

The king's gaze moved to her sword. "The damsel carries Excalibur!" he said in surprise.

"That's right, Your Majesty," Rhianna said. "I've come for the Grail of Stars. Is it here?"

The king sighed. "So this time, men send an innocent young girl to seek what they dare not. The best thing you can do, my dear, is get back on that ship right now, and forget you ever heard of the Grail of Stars. Galahad here will return you safely to wherever he found you."

Rhianna tightened her hand on Excalibur's hilt. She didn't want to hurt the frail old king, but she hadn't come this far to be packed off home like a child. "No one sent me. I came of my own free will to find the Grail to wake my father, and I'm not going back without it."

The grey-cloaked guardians stiffened. There was a hiss down the lines as arrows magically appeared on their bowstrings. Rhianna's heart pounded. Out of the corner of her eye, she saw Cai grip his lance tighter. Arianrhod hugged the pack containing the Crown to her chest. Gareth ducked behind a wall, then remembered he was a ghost and stood in front of the arrows with his arms spread, grinning.

Sir Bors quickly stepped forward to join Rhianna and cleared his throat. "I'm sorry, Your

Majesty. The girl gets carried away sometimes. But if your guardians hurt her, they'll have Arthur's knights to answer to." He dropped his hand to his sword too.

The arrows swung round to take aim at the big knight.

"Enough!" The king held up a blue-veined hand, and the archers relaxed. "Forgive my guardians. They are rather jumpy lately. Something is happening in the mists. I sense a darkness between the worlds, where light once shone. I hoped Lancelot would come, but I see the Lance of Truth has come without him." He frowned at Cai. "Is Arthur's champion so besotted with Queen Guinevere, he's sent his squire in his place?"

"Sir Lancelot wanted to come," Rhianna said, remembering guiltily how she had left the silver-haired knight at Nimue's lake with the queen. "But I stopped him."

The king blinked at her. "And who are you, damsel, to order grown men around and carry Arthur's sword at your hip like a knight?" He smiled. "Or almost like a knight. I see you've got it on the wrong side."

Rhianna glanced down at her scabbard, which she wore on her right hip so that she could draw her sword left-handed. But she did not adjust it. She had learned her lesson the hard way, fighting dragons.

"She's Rhianna Pendragon, King Arthur's daughter!" Cai said proudly. "She's better with that sword left-handed than any of his knights. And I'm Sir Cai, her champion. So before anyone touches her, they'll have to fight *me*." He swung the Lance of Truth at the nearest guardians, who jumped back warily. Gareth winced as the shaft sparkled through his ghostly body, and glared at Cai.

"Enough, Cai!" Sir Bors said. "Put up that lance before you skewer someone. We're among friends here – the Fisher King must welcome all those who come on a Grail Quest, isn't that right Your Majesty?"

The king nodded thoughtfully and gave Rhianna a closer look. "She's Arthur's daughter? Really? Where has such a fierce damsel been hiding all these years?"

"On Avalon," Cai said, still scowling.

"Explaining the fairy horses, I suppose," the king said. "Did this young damsel come out of Avalon, too?" He lifted Arianrhod's hair to see her face, but hissed through his teeth when he saw the pentacle scar on the maid's cheek.

"She bears the witch-mark!"

Arianrhod shrank back as the arrows swung round again, this time aiming at her.

"Morgan Le Fay did that to her, but she's my maid now," Rhianna said quickly, shrugging off Sir Bors' hand to step between her friend and the arrows. "Arianrhod was born right here in your castle, Your Majesty, so you needn't be afraid of her."

The king frowned. "Morgan Le Fay... now, that's a name I haven't heard in a while. I'd hoped never to hear it again. Is the witch still alive?"

"Not exactly," Rhianna said. She shuddered when she thought of Lady Morgan's ghost, which sometimes still appeared in her dreams.

"She's in Annwn now," Sir Bors explained. "The Crown of Dreams killed her, like it killed her son, Mordred, last year."

"Or not," Gareth muttered.

"Have you brought the Crown of Dreams, too?" the king said, his eyes gleaming.

"It's in here, Your Majesty," Arianrhod whispered, hugging her pack tightly.

"The Sword, the Lance, the Crown, and three youngsters to carry them... I can see there's more to this quest than meets the eye." The king smiled. "You must be weary after your long journey. Come into my hall and tell me your story over some refreshment. The princess must cleanse herself and prepare to meet my queen." He looked at Rhianna again and shook his head. "King Arthur's daughter on a Grail Quest, who would have believed it?"

They entered the castle under an archway of blue and green lights. The king led Sir Bors and Cai away, while four of the grey-cloaked guardians escorted Rhianna and Arianrhod to a pool that was open to the night sky. It looked big enough to swim in and had been beautifully tiled with underwater scenes. Stars reflected in the steaming water and flowers grew around the edge, scenting the air.

Rhianna eyed the water, reluctant to remove her armour and sword in this strange castle. "You bathe," she told her friend, jumping up on one of the marble benches. "I'll keep watch."

Arianrhod folded her arms. "I'm not letting you attend a feast at the Grail Castle smelling of horse! If they wanted to kill us, they could have done so already back there on the quay."

"I'd like to have seen them try," Rhianna

said loudly, peering between the lights. She could just make out the shadowy forms of their grey-cloaked escort standing guard around the pool.

"Where are our friends?" she called.

"Bathing with the men, Princess," the nearest guardian said without turning round. "In the Fisher King's castle, damsels and knights do not bathe together. You're perfectly safe, don't worry. We shall not peep."

Rhianna scowled at the grey-cloaked back. To test this claim, she drew Excalibur and sprang off the bench.

The guardian tensed as her blade whispered past his ear.

"You were looking!" she accused.

"I heard you jump off the bench, Princess," said the guardian. "But I have orders not to hurt you, so if you wish to kill me then go ahead. No one will stop you. But we do not shed blood in this castle."

Rhianna slid Excalibur back into its scabbard with a sigh. She wasn't about to blood her blade now, not after keeping it clean for so long. Except for her own blood, when the Sword had briefly been in Mordred's hands last year, not a drop had soiled Excalibur's blade since she'd won the sword from Lady Nimue at the very start of her quest.

"No," she said. "I'm keeping my blade clean so I can take Excalibur back to Avalon for my father."

"Glad to hear it," the guardian said with a smile, and Rhianna got the feeling that she had passed some kind of test. Slim fingers reached up, the grey hood dropped, and she found herself looking at a girl not much older than herself. The guardian laughed at Rhianna's surprised expression. "You're not the only damsel who can fight, Princess," she said.

"Come on in, my lady!" Arianrhod called. "The water's lovely, and there are fish in here as well… they tickle when they nibble your toes!"

Rhianna gave in. She took off her armour and folded it neatly, leaving it beside the pool with their packs. She laid Excalibur in its red scabbard over the top, so she could grab her sword easily if need be. Then she slipped into the water to join Arianrhod.

While they were bathing, a girl appeared with two white dresses and laid them on the bench. She placed two crowns of white flowers on top and gathered up their dirty clothes. But when the girl picked up the armour, Rhianna sprang out of the water and snatched up Excalibur again.

"Don't touch that!" she said.

The girl dropped the armour at once. "I'm sorry, Princess, but I thought you might like it cleaned?"

"It doesn't need cleaning," Rhianna said. "It was made in Avalon, so it's magic. It cleans itself."

"What about these?" the girl dangled her riding leggings and tunic at arm's length. Even Rhianna had to admit they stank. The thought of putting them back on now she had bathed made her itch. But she might need to fight.

"Leave them – they'll be fine," she said, pulling a face at the dresses. "You can wash Arianrhod's clothes and clean my boots for me, but I'm keeping my armour and my sword!"

"Of course, Princess," said the girl, giving her a dazzling smile. "Only our queen can clean your sword."

"That's not quite true," Rhianna muttered. "Lady Nimue cleaned it after my father fought Mordred..." But the girl had already vanished through one of the archways.

Rhianna frowned after her, while Arianrhod chewed her lip.

"I'm not used to people waiting on me," the maid whispered, looking at the white dress the girl had left for her. "What am I going to wear? That gown is much too fine for me."

"No it isn't," Rhianna said firmly. "And you'll look much nicer than me in white, with your dark hair and skin. You were born here don't forget. You wouldn't have been a maid if you'd stayed. Maybe you'd have been a princess."

Arianrhod shook her head as they both got dressed. "Oh no, my lady. I'm no princess. And I'm glad my mother left me at Camelot, or I would never have met you. Now sit still, and let me do your hair."

While they waited, Rhianna reluctantly let her friend arrange her hair in tumbling copper curls over her armour. The boots came back smelling of fish oil, but she pulled them on thankfully. Before Arianrhod could protest, she picked up one of the flower crowns and settled it on her friend's head.

"There!" she said. "A proper princess!"

She said it to make her friend feel better. But Arianrhod did look beautiful, standing by the star-filled pool with the flowers glowing in her dark hair.

The maid shyly picked up the other flower

crown and hesitated. "This doesn't feel right, my lady," she whispered. "You should be the special one at this feast. I know what might work with your armour…"

Rhianna buckled Excalibur back around her waist, while Arianrhod rummaged in her pack. At first she thought her friend was after some bit of jewellery she'd brought along. Then she saw the green glitter in her hand.

"Oh no," she said. "No, Arianrhod, I can't wear *that* crown tonight."

"Yes, you must! It's perfect. All bright colours, and the green jewel at the front will match your eyes. Besides, you might need it when you take your Grail test." She settled the Crown of Dreams on Rhianna's damp hair and stepped back with a satisfied smile. "That's much better!"

Rhianna tensed, expecting to feel the familiar heat from the jewels. But the Crown sat lightly on her head, and even the Jewel of Annwn only glowed gently. She touched it, and sighed when her fingers came away cool. Maybe the third Light was less dangerous in the Grail Castle? And Arianrhod was right – it might give her an advantage when she took the test of the Grail.

"All right," she said. "But only until I've been presented to the queen. I'm not wearing this crown all night. I need to be awake to get the Grail, not go off on another spirit ride with the dragon. If you see me falling asleep, pinch me."

Arianrhod nodded.

"Hard, mind!" Rhianna added. "You've seen what this Crown can do, and Elphin's not here this time to wake me with his harp."

Her friend bit her lip at the reminder, and promised she would try.

Their escort materialised from the shadows and looked them up and down. If the guardians disapproved of Rhianna's armour, they did not say anything. "Ready, Princess?" asked the one she'd threatened earlier with Excalibur.

She had never felt less ready in her life. But she drew a deep breath and nodded.

⚜

Rhianna had attended Lord Avallach's feasts in Avalon, where the Avalonians danced all night and made song pictures in the crystal walls of his palace. She had seen Camelot's Great Hall decorated with blossoms at midsummer, and with holly and candles to celebrate Christ's mass at midwinter. But she'd never seen anything like this.

She paused at the entrance to catch her breath. The hall of the Grail Castle turned out to be a huge sea-cave. Blue and green lights twinkled across the soaring arches like stars. A pool occupied most of the floor, the lights reflected in its depths. Tables set with food and drink floated slowly around the pool. The Fisher King's people sat on steps around the edge with their legs in the water, chattering and laughing as they ate. White doves fluttered overhead. The guardians in their grey cloaks melted into the shadows, and Rhianna saw more tunnels leading from the cave deep into the island.

The maidens all wore white dresses and white flower crowns like Arianrhod, who lifted her chin a little when she realised she was not the only one dressed so finely. The knights wore dazzling white tunics. She spotted Sir Bors looking uncomfortable, with a grease stain already visible on his.

Cai stood self-consciously near the pool holding the Lance of Truth, which cast a glittering blue reflection in the water. He waved to them in relief. Rhianna slid Excalibur a short way out of its scabbard and saw its blade shining too. Magic. She quickly slid the sword back again. But she could do nothing about the Crown, which had sensed the enchantment of the Grail Castle and begun to glow.

Coloured sparks flew from her head as she walked towards the pool. The dancers all turned to stare at her. She heard a few whisper 'Arthur's daughter' and 'Grail Quest'.

Others shielded their eyes. Rhianna saw Sir Galahad chatting with another ghostly young knight. A shiver went down her spine as they turned to look at her too.

Arianrhod hesitated. "I think that's Sir Percival," she whispered. "He died on his quest like Galahad did, but nobody knows how."

Rhianna didn't need the reminder. She grasped her friend's hand and pulled her on. She marched up to the pool and hissed at Cai, "Well, go on then. Announce me."

Cai was mouthing something at them, pointing urgently at the water. When Rhianna glared at him, he cleared his throat, banged the Lance on the floor and said, "Princess Rhianna Pendragon, Your Majesties!"

The king climbed to his feet and nodded in approval at the Crown on Rhianna's head.

He frowned slightly as his gaze travelled down to her armour and the Sword strapped around her waist, but smiled and said, "Welcome, Princess! Come feast with us, and we shall see if the Grail judges you good enough to drink from it. Sit beside my queen down there. She'll look after you now."

One of the women seated at the pool looked round, and Rhianna froze. She'd expected the queen to be old like her husband, and had assumed her hair would be silver, reflecting the green and blue lights like the king's. But when she saw gills open and close on the slender neck, Rhianna knew she'd made a mistake. The Queen of the Grail Castle was ageless and beautiful. She had green hair and turquoise eyes and, splashing in the starlit water, a beautiful fish's tail.

Rhianna felt dizzy. The Fisher King's strange name... the ship appearing at the enchanted lake where she had won Excalibur from its fish-tailed guardian... the same fish-lady who had helped them get the Lance of Truth from Mordred... Suddenly, everything fell into place. Who else had been testing her from the very start of her quest?

"Lady Nimue!" she breathed.

◄◙ 6 ◙►

Rhianna's Test

Only the bravest drink from the Grail,
Many a knight has tried and failed.
When a damsel feasts with the Fisher Queen
Then will the final secret be seen.

Lady Nimue smiled. "Welcome, Rhianna
Pendragon! You took your time, but you're
here now – and with three of the Lights, which
is more than Arthur's knights ever brought me.
You've done better than I expected. Come and
join us." She patted the step beside her.

With a start, Rhianna realised that at least half of the people sitting around the pool, feasting from the king's floating tables, had fish-tails like Lady Nimue – *Queen* Nimue. That would take some getting used to.

"But how... How did you get here?" she asked.

The last time she'd seen Nimue was on the bridge below Camelot, when the fish-lady had been washed downriver by Mordred's conjured flood. No wonder they hadn't found her in her lake. Though, now she came to think about it, Nimue always had known a lot more than she should do for a water spirit trapped in an enchanted wood.

"I swam, of course." Nimue said with another smile. "Water connects all worlds. Are you ready for your final test?"

Rhianna descended the steps and eyed the pool warily. Everyone was watching her.

"What test?" she asked. "Do I have to swim with you again? Because it's going to be a bit difficult in my armour, and I'm not removing it again – last time I did that, one of your maidens tried to take it."

Nimue smiled again. "You know what I'm going to ask, Rhianna Pendragon. My final riddle, the one you couldn't answer when I asked you before. You remember it, don't you?"

Rhianna froze. "*What does the Grail contain?*" she whispered.

Nimue nodded. "A question many men have died over. If you drink and answer correctly, then you may take the Grail from this place and use it as you wish. Wrong, and it may kill you too. Are you ready?"

A hush fell over the cavern as the fish-lady lifted a battered silver cup from its floating table and filled it with clear liquid from a flask. The cup smoked slightly as she held it out to Rhianna. Sir Bors frowned.

Rhianna did not move, her eyes fixed on the goblet. Was that it? The Grail of Stars? It looked so ordinary, apart from the liquid Nimue had poured into it. She remembered Sir Galahad's warning. *Be careful what you drink in the Grail Castle.*

"If you're afraid, you can always feast at the king's table instead. You won't be the first to refuse the test." Nimue's turquoise gaze rested on Sir Bors, who wiped crumbs from his tunic and flushed.

Sir Galahad and Sir Percival were watching her more eagerly than the rest. Galahad whispered something to his friend, and the other ghost chuckled. Gareth, hovering nearby, clutched his throat and pretended to choke.

"Careful, Damsel Rhianna," Sir Bors warned.

"I'm not afraid!" Rhianna said.

Before she had a chance to think about it too much, she seized the cup from Nimue and took a brave swallow. White fire burned all the way into her stomach.

She closed her eyes until the burning stopped, and found herself sitting on the step between Nimue and another fish-lady, with her legs in the water and Excalibur's scabbard trailing in the pool. The other fish-people swam across to stop her falling in. Suddenly, it seemed a very good place to be.

"What does the Grail contain?" Lady Nimue asked again, taking the cup from

Rhianna's numb fingers and setting it safely back on the table. She ran her webbed hand around the jewels in Rhianna's crown. "Do you see the answer yet, Rhianna Pendragon? Maybe it's in one of these pretty jewels hiding their Pendragon secrets? Why not take a look?"

The Crown warmed under her touch, and Excalibur shone brighter. Light flashed from Nimue's cup until the whole cavern filled with rainbows. Rhianna heard Cai gasp as the Lance of Truth flashed with colour, too.

She thought of Elphin's words, before he'd ridden out for the Lonely Tor. *I'm not sure what'll happen when all four Lights come together.* Using the Crown to look for the answer to Nimue's riddle no longer seemed like such a good idea. Panicking, she tried to get up. The Lights were meant to come together in

Avalon to wake her father, not here... Then her head shattered with colour and light, and pictures magically formed in the glittering surface of the pool.

King Arthur knighting Mordred with Excalibur...

The shadrake shrieking over the battlefield...

Her cousin swinging his axe with two hands towards the king's head...

Her father's body lying in the bottom of Merlin's boat, covered by the Pendragon shield—

She snatched off the Crown with trembling hands and flung it into the pool, destroying the images that shimmered there. "Enough! I already know all that. Make it show me the answer to your riddle, or I'm not wearing it again."

She didn't want her family's secrets reflected

in the pool for all at the feast to see, like song-pictures in the walls of Lord Avallach's crystal palace. What if the Crown showed everyone the secret of dragon riding next, and some heroic fool tried to do it?

Lady Nimue dived gracefully into the pool and retrieved the Crown of Dreams. She gave Rhianna a sympathetic look. "I know it's painful for you to remember your father's death, but there's more here – something buried deep, a secret nobody wants you to see. I'll help you, shall I?" She replaced the crown on Rhianna's head.

Rhianna's limbs felt heavy, and her sword weighed her down. She nearly slipped off the step into the depths of the pool. The fish-people's webbed hands gripped her sword belt and held her tightly. *A secret nobody wanted her to see...* Morgan Le Fay had worn this Crown in Dragonland before it killed her. Had the witch sabotaged it so that Rhianna would not be able to use it to gain the fourth Light?

"Damsel Rhianna!" Cai called from a long way off, but she didn't even have the strength to turn her head and tell him she was all right, she was just searching for the answer to the riddle of the Grail.

Nimue rejoined them on the steps and pushed Rhianna's head down into her scaled lap. "Don't fight the magic," she whispered, stroking her hair. "Now, let's see what the Crown of Dreams was trying to tell us, shall we?"

Rhianna tried to make the Crown show her the answer to Nimue's riddle, but now she could feel the dark magic working against her. The fish-people's webbed hands held her firmly, and the jewels grew warm again.

A shadow formed in the light over the pool, and more pictures appeared in the water.

Morgan Le Fay, young and beautiful with oak leaves in her hair, dancing in a druid grove...

Merlin in his man's body showing the witch how to use the spiral pathfinder on the end of his staff... the shadrake shrieking as the sly Morgan kissed her surprised tutor...

A baby born in blood and shadow...

Mordred as a small boy, laughing while his witch mother drew her dagger and cut a pentacle into the pale cheek of her young maid...

Seeing her younger self reflected in the pool, Arianrhod screamed. "Rhia!"

Her friend's cry broke through the visions. Rhianna groped for her sword. As soon as her hand touched Excalibur's hilt, some of her strength returned. She drew the blade awkwardly, and the fish-people dived into the pool to avoid it, releasing her belt. She scrabbled backwards around the steps and lifted the sword two-handed, looking for an enemy, its blade wobbling between her and Lady Nimue.

Through sparkling stars, she saw Sir Bors struggling with a knot of grey-cloaked guardians, who were trying to disarm the big knight and march him from the hall. She blinked to clear her vision and saw more of the guardians closing in on Cai, who swung the Lance in a wild circle to keep them at bay.

"They've poisoned Princess Rhianna!" the boy yelled.

"What did you give her?" Sir Bors shouted at the fish-queen. "What was in that cup?"

The guardians did not seem to consider Arianrhod a threat. Before they could stop her, the maid pushed past them and jumped into the pool. With her white dress swirling around her, she splashed across to the floating table, snatched up the cup Rhianna had drunk from, and flung it across the cave. White light flashed out of it, and everyone – ghosts as well as the living – ducked.

Arianrhod stared down at her hands in surprise. They shone like Sir Galahad's had when Rhianna summoned his ghost to the Round Table. But Excalibur and the Lance dimmed, and the Crown grew cooler on Rhianna's head. She blinked in relief as the pictures in the pool faded. She felt stupid letting Arianrhod talk her into wearing it in the first place. Of course the answer she sought

was not hidden in the Pendragon jewels –
otherwise her father would have told his
knights the correct answer so they could bring
him the Grail, instead of dying on their quests!

The maid looked in horror at the goblet
she'd thrown. It rolled up against the rock near
one of the tunnels, where its glimmer slowly
faded.

"Did I break it?" she whispered. "Oh, I'm
sorry…"

Lady Nimue sighed. "You broke the magic,
that's for sure. No matter, I've seen enough."
She frowned at Arianrhod. "Well don't just
stand there, child. Go and pick up that cup. It
takes more than a few dents to break a grail.
Galahad will show you where to put it. And you
can put your sword away, Rhianna Pendragon.
You haven't passed my test, but it seems you're

made of sterner stuff than most of Arthur's knights so at least you'll live. I shouldn't be surprised. You grew up in Avalon, after all. My guardians will show you to your room, where you can sleep off my potion in peace."

"You didn't have to trick her like that!" Sir Bors yelled, tugging at the hands that held him. "I should have guessed what you meant to do, luring the poor girl here with your quests and your riddles, just so you could take a sneaky look at the secrets in the Pendragon Crown! You're worse than Morgan Le Fay, using an innocent girl for your own ends. Are you sure you're all right, Damsel Rhianna?"

Rhianna felt terrible, but she managed to stagger up the steps without dropping Excalibur. "Let Sir Bors and Cai go," she ordered, swinging her blade at the nearest guardians, who were a blur of grey cloaks.

The guardians looked at their queen, who raised a webbed hand to stay them.

"What do you want me to do with this, my lady?" Arianrhod called, nervously edging past the guardians to pick up the Grail from where it had rolled against the wall. No longer shining, it looked like an ordinary battered cup again. But the magic they'd seen earlier said different.

"Put it in my pack," Rhianna told her.

"Put it where Galahad shows you," Nimue corrected.

Rhianna squeezed her eyes shut. The cavern spun, and her ears rang with a sound that reminded her of Elphin's broken harp.

"Arianrhod, put it in my pack and GO!" she said.

Her friend hesitated.

"Arianrhod," Lady Nimue snapped. "You're the daughter of a Grail maiden. I won't tell you again. Take that cup out of here, before it does kill somebody."

The maid looked in anguish at Rhianna. Nimue impatiently waved two of the guardians towards the girl. Desperate to keep her friend free, Rhianna leaped between them and told the guardians, "It's all right, she'll do it." Then she winked at Arianrhod and whispered, "You'd better do what she says, *but remember our trick with Excalibur at the North Wall.*"

Arianrhod gave her a puzzled glance. Then she understood. Ducking her head to hide her smile, she clutched the cup to her chest and hurried out of the hall after Sir Galahad's ghost. Gareth, who had been at the North Wall with them, grinned at Rhianna and followed.

As they passed Cai, the Lance flared brightly. Cai gave a yell of surprise and dropped it. One of the grey-cloaked guardians picked it up. The others closed around the boy, seized his arms and dragged him out of the hall after Sir Bors.

"Get off me!" he yelled, kicking them. "If your fish-queen hurts Damsel Rhianna, I'll come back and kill you all, I swear it on my knightly oath!"

The cavern spun around Rhianna. The pool glittered with stars. Her sword grew heavier. Her arms lowered, and the blade clanged against the rock at her feet.

A guardian gently took Excalibur from her numb fingers, and two more ran to catch her as her legs gave way. The Fisher King bent over her and removed her crown.

"It's nearly daylight," he said with a sigh. "This castle sleeps by day. Sweet dreams, Princess. It's no shame to fail the test. At least you get to sail home with your life."

Rhianna fought to stay awake. "Please, sire, you've got to let me take the Grail of Stars to Avalon!" she begged. "You've got to, or my father will never return to Camelot. I'll bring it straight back here afterwards, I promise... or throw it into Queen Nimue's lake when I've finished with it, whatever you like."

"Even if you'd passed the test, I'm afraid we can't let you take the Grail from this place, Rhianna Pendragon," Lady Nimue called from the pool. "I hate to disappoint such a brave damsel, but it seems Merlin has not told you the whole truth. I think he sent you here to try for the Grail because he knew he would not survive such a quest himself. Druids play the long game. He tried to get hold of it before by sending Arthur's knights after it, and failed. He's betrayed us. The Crown does not lie. You saw the visions too. He might even have been working with Morgan Le Fay all along to put Prince Mordred on the throne."

"That's a lie!" Rhianna said.

Her heart pounded and she felt so dizzy she could barely focus on the fish-lady, let alone think straight. Most of the lights in the cavern had flickered out when Arianrhod threw the goblet, and everyone else – humans, ghosts and fish-people – seemed to have gone. Darkness arched over her, reminding her of the shadrake's lair, where Mordred had left her to die during her quest for the Crown of Dreams.

I failed, she thought.

"Merlin hates Mordred," she said. "He'd never help him or his witch-mother... why should he?"

Lady Nimue's tinkling laugh reached her. "Because, Rhianna Pendragon, Merlin taught Morgan Le Fay magic when she was a girl. She used to be very beautiful. It appears none can resist Lady Morgan's charms, not even a great druid like Merlin. I wasn't sure before, but the four Lights together can reveal even those truths hidden from the world by the darkest magic. It seems your cousin Mordred has druid blood as well as Pendragon blood. Prince Mordred is Merlin's son."

DARK FAMILY

Mordred bent over the Avalonian prince, whose limp body his men had finally fished out of the water. Seaweed was tangled in his dark curls. The violet eyes stared up at the Tor, blank and unseeing. Silver gleamed through a rip in the boy's tunic. Mordred closed his gauntlet about the druid spiral the prince wore on a cord around his neck and jerked it free. He'd been slightly disappointed to find the rider of the fairy horse wasn't his cousin, but at least he now had the means to get to Avalon.

He turned to his captain, who held his

other captive flapping upside down by its jesses. "Bring that stubborn merlin over here."

He thrust the spiral towards the bird. "Recognise this, druid?" he said. "This is the pathfinder from the end of your old staff. I know you can use it to open the mists between worlds. If you help me and my men get to Avalon, I'll let Gareth's snivelling mother try to revive the fairy lad. I'm sure I can think of a use for him when my cousin arrives."

The merlin screeched at him and tried to peck his hand.

"Very well, then," Mordred said in frustration. "We'll see how long it takes a fairy to drown."

"Oh, don't be so mean, Merlin!" called a sweet voice from behind them. "You could give Mordred a little help, for once."

Mordred, who had been about to kick the Avalonian's body back into the water, whirled round. Morgan Le Fay's ghost sat on the end of the jetty. She was weaving a net in her lap from lengths of glowing green rope.

He scowled at her. "How long have you been sitting there?" One drawback of his shadow-eyes was that he no longer needed the dark mirror to see his dead mother. And she had a habit of turning up at the most inconvenient moments.

"Long enough," the witch said. "Avalonians don't die as easily as men, foolish boy! If you return that body to the water, the prince might find a way to warn your cousin you're waiting for her. Here, bind him with this. It'll keep him quiet until you decide what to do with him."

She tossed him a length of the green rope.

While his bloodbeards bound the slender wrists, Morgan Le Fay joined them and ran a ghostly finger down the merlin's breast.

"Ah, my dear Merlin," the witch said. "Such a fragile little body you've ended up in, but it doesn't have to be this way. Arthur's hot-headed daughter has already proved she cares nothing for the Lights themselves – only for her friends, her love-struck mother and her dear departed father. That's girls for you. She's reached the Grail Castle, you know. She'll be dead by morning. Whereas Prince Mordred here is no longer trapped in the body Arthur crippled for him at Camlann. You could work with him as you once worked with Arthur. Then if the king's daughter somehow survives her quest, we could marry them and breed a child with both druid and Pendragon blood, raised by us to rule over the kingdoms of men, Avalon and Annwn. Just think… you and me, with all four Lights at our command! You could take any body you liked, then. Get rid of old Avallach and live in his crystal palace, if you wish. What a team we'd make!"

Her eyes gleamed. The merlin went still.

Mordred stared at her.

"Enough, Mother!" he said, his stomach fluttering in alarm. "*I'm* going to be the one who controls the four Lights and sits on Arthur's throne. Men will follow *me!* You promised. Besides, I don't want to marry my cousin, and she hasn't got any druid blood… has she?"

If his cousin could work magic like

Merlin, he'd be in trouble if she actually did manage to get hold of the Grail of Stars.

His bloodbeards coughed and shuffled their feet. Gareth's mother picked seaweed out of the Avalonian boy's curls, shuddering as the enchanted ropes worked their magic and all colour drained from the captive's face.

Morgan le Fay laughed. "See what a monster we've bred, Merlin? Druid blood doesn't run in *Rhianna's* veins, silly boy – how could it, a daughter of Arthur and Guinevere? You're the one with the magic, my son. Why do you think you're standing here, strong and whole, with only a rotten fist to keep your spirit tethered to the world of men? You'd have been in Annwn long ago, otherwise. The truth is Merlin's your father, however much he might regret it now. He found me very attractive once – didn't you, my dear?"

Mordred's head spun, and he tightened his gauntlet about the pathfinder. All this time he'd thought he was the son of a dark lord summoned by his mother from Annwn – his only consolation when the other boys at Camelot had called him a 'fatherless brat'. Who'd have thought it? The son of Merlin, greatest of the druids!

"Why didn't you tell me?" he demanded, eyeing the little hawk. It looked as uncomfortable as he felt. "You let me grow up fatherless!"

The witch regarded him in amusement. "And have the truth reach Arthur's ears? Exactly how long do you think my dear brother would have let us stay at Camelot? Even Merlin never guessed for sure."

Mordred slowly unclenched his fist, seeing the possibilities. "Druid blood… you mean I can use magic to protect myself?"

"You already have," his mother said, with another of her silvery laughs. "Unless someone burns your mortal fist, of course. Fire will finish even those who can work the strongest enchantments."

Mordred looked at his gauntlet and felt sick all over again.

"And the spirit transfer," he said. "Like the druids do when their old body dies. Can I do that?"

"If you wish," said his mother. "Though I wouldn't advise it unless you really have no choice… Not so easy, is it, Merlin? The stronger the body the harder it fights, as Merlin here found out with my shadrake."

The merlin launched itself at the witch, claws outstretched. But the leash attached to his jesses tugged him back.

Morgan Le Fay laughed. "Temper, temper," she said. "Merlin thinks I tricked him, which maybe I did. But it's time to put our differences aside for the common good, and get rid of Arthur's daughter before she takes the Grail to Avalon and wakes the king from his enchanted sleep so he can take his revenge upon us all."

The merlin glared at her, and Morgan Le Fay sighed.

"Admit it, my dear, you're just as scared as we are. If she survives the test of the Grail, Arthur's daughter will soon be on her way to Avalon, bringing at least three of the Lights with her. When the Lights come together, you know as well as I do that the old ways will change, and our time will be over. If by some miracle the girl brings the Grail of Stars as well, that'll put all four Lights in Lord Avallach's hands, and who knows what the fairy lord plans to do with that kind of power, once Arthur is awake?"

She stroked her green net thoughtfully. "Rhianna trusts the Avalonian lord. That's your fault, Merlin, but now's your chance to make up for it. We can't let the world be swallowed up by the enchanted mists while the Wild Hunt rides at will, snatching men's souls and turning us all into Avallach's slaves. These ropes will hold the girl as tightly as they hold her fairy prince. All we need is someone she trusts to lead her into our trap."

She smiled at the merlin in a way that

reminded Mordred of how she used to smile at him when he'd been small. "Tell your captain to let the bird go," she said.

Reluctantly, Mordred passed on the instruction. He scowled as the little falcon darted off into the mist with a final screech.

"But what if the druid betrays us…?"

"Doesn't matter." Morgan Le Fay knelt to close the Avalonian boy's violet eyes. "Merlin will be back for his pathfinder, and the girl's not going to stay away for much longer once she hears we've got her Avalonian prince."

7

Escape

Ghosts stood guard while the castle slept
And a maiden for her princess wept.
An empty cup might be easy to hide
But can it cross the water wide?

Rhianna ran along dripping tunnels searching for the Grail of Stars. Whatever she had drunk from Lady Nimue's cup had made her dizzy, and her legs were joining together into a fish's tail. She had to find the fourth Light before they finished transforming, but she did not know where to look.

She came to a winding stair and began to climb, her half-changed legs trembling at every step. King Arthur's ghost stood at the top, holding a cup filled with dazzling light. When he saw her coming, he smiled and lifted the cup to his lips.

"No, Father!" she screamed. "Don't drink – it's poison!"

She tried to knock the cup from his hands. But her new tail flopped uselessly on the steps, and she slipped back down. Her father swallowed, and the cup fell from his grasp. Its contents spilled down the stairs in a foaming wave, swept Rhianna up and washed her back down the tower. She thrashed her tail, desperately trying to keep her head above the shining liquid. It would kill her, so she mustn't swallow… mustn't swallow…

"My lady? Rhia, wake up! It's only a dream."

Rhianna's hand knocked against something metallic, and cold liquid splashed her skin. She jerked awake to see Arianrhod's anxious face peering down at her. Her heart steadied. She took deep breaths.

She lay on a bed in a chamber hung with tapestries that reminded her of the Damsel Tower at Camelot. Mist swirled at the windows, filling the room with grey light. Her friend held a battered silver cup, which Rhianna must have spilled as she woke. A wet stain was spreading over the bedcover, which had tangled around her legs. She kicked free of the clinging material with a shudder.

Only a dream. She stared at the cup in

Arianrhod's hand, a shiver of memory going down her spine. It looked like the one Nimue had offered her at the feast, except it had a new dent in one side.

"Is that what I think it is?" she said, hoping her friend had understood what she'd asked her to do.

The maid blushed. "You did tell me to put it in your pack, Rhia. When Sir Galahad showed me where to put it after the feast, there were hundreds of other goblets, a whole cavern of them glittering in the dark. He wouldn't go inside, so it was easy to switch them. I hid this one under my skirt and moved one of the others to the shelf where it belongs – I made sure I dropped the other one first to give it a new dent, which was a lot easier than making that look-alike Excalibur when we played our trick on Mordred at the North Wall! But it's just some old cup without Lady Nimue's magic drink inside... are you sure you want it? We've got plenty of prettier ones back at Camelot."

It's the Grail of Stars, silly! Rhianna wanted to say. But she frowned. In the daylight, it did indeed look like a very ordinary cup. No white light, as she'd seen at the feast last night. No foaming poison, as there had been in her dream. She wasn't even sure any more that it was real silver.

She swung her legs to the floor and checked them, relieved to see no sign of scales. With another wave of relief, she saw her Avalonian armour neatly folded at the end of the bed, next to Excalibur in its red scabbard. The Crown of Dreams lay on top, but her father's ghost had gone.

"Only a dream," she whispered.

"My lady?" Arianrhod set down the empty cup, which wobbled on its dented base.

Rhianna laughed. This cup was the Grail of Stars, the fourth Light with the power to bring someone back from the dead? No wonder her father's knights had failed to find it.

She drew Excalibur from its scabbard to check the blade. Satisfied the sword hadn't been harmed, she dressed quickly and sprang to the door. But it refused to open.

"I'm afraid it's locked, my lady," Arianrhod said in an apologetic tone. "But at least they let me stay with you. I was so scared. You kept thrashing about and screaming in your sleep... I thought you were going to die like Sir Galahad and the others."

"Don't be silly." Rhianna scowled at the door.

"Lady Nimue just wanted to see the secrets in the Crown of Dreams. She didn't want to kill me."

It must have been a strong potion to bring on such visions, though. She frowned, trying to remember how much had been real, which had been memories from the Crown, and what had been part of her dream. She remembered Nimue saying something about Merlin being Mordred's father. She shook her head. The fish-lady must have made a mistake – Merlin was on their side, even if he hadn't been of much use lately.

"What happened to Cai and Sir Bors?" she asked. "Did you see where the guardians took them?"

"No, my lady. I'm sorry."

Rhianna sighed. "We have to get out of

here and find them. How far up are we?" She leaned out of the window and peered down into a silver mist.

"I don't know," Arianrhod said. "This castle's very confusing, but we went up a lot of steps so I don't think we're near the fish-people any more."

"Good." Rhianna looked for something to throw out of the window. Her gaze settled on the dented Grail. She shook her head and grabbed an apple from the fruit bowl instead. She dropped the apple into the mist and held her breath, listening.

Arianrhod pressed against her shoulder, listening too.

Just when Rhianna wondered if the apple had landed on something too soft to make a noise, they heard a faint splash below followed by an eager whinny.

This is a very sweet apple! came her mist horse's faint voice. *Can we go home now?*

"Alba!" Rhianna put a leg over the sill.

"No, my lady!" Arianrhod grabbed her arm and pulled her back inside. "What if you land on a rock and break your neck?"

Rhianna frowned.

"Are there any rocks down there, beautiful one?" she called down to the mare.

There are many sharp stones, Alba reported. *Evenstar does not like it here. He misses his rider. But we hide like you say. We go home now?* The mare sounded hopeful.

With a sigh, Rhianna drew her leg back inside. Even if she missed the rocks and did not break any bones when she landed, Arianrhod would never jump after her. She could try to get back inside and let her maid out of the door. But this castle was meant to be enchanted. Sir Lancelot hadn't been able to get back in to see Lady Elaine and his baby son. Even if she had the Grail now, she couldn't abandon her friends.

"Wait a bit longer, my beautiful one!" she called down. "We'll come as soon as we can."

Arianrhod looked relieved. "How about we summon someone?" she said. Before Rhianna could stop her, the maid had picked up the dented Grail and was banging it against the door, shouting for the guards.

"No!" Rhianna grabbed the cup. "Don't bash that about. You might destroy the magic. Put it in your pack. They won't hear unless they're waiting outside, anyway. I've got a better idea."

She straightened her shoulders, rested her hand on Excalibur's hilt and closed her eyes.

Finding the right knightly spirit was easy this time – the sword's magic was strong in this place.

"Open this door at once, Sir Galahad!" she yelled with battle-trained lungs. "I know you can hear me. By the power of the Sword of Light that was forged in Avalon and your knightly oath made to my father King Arthur, I command you to let us out!"

There was a pause long enough to make her wonder what she'd do if the knight did not come. Then Sir Galahad's ghost rippled through the solid door. He smiled to see Rhianna awake and dressed.

"No need to shout, Princess. The dead are not deaf, you know." He gave the Crown a curious look. "Did you have any more visions?"

Rhianna scowled at him. "That's Pendragon

business. Unlock this door and let us out, will you?"

"Sorry, Princess. I can't do that," Galahad said.

She tightened her grip on Excalibur and scowled again. "My father knighted you with this sword, so you must obey the Pendragon who holds it, unless I unknight you like I unknighted Mordred. I can do that, you know."

"I know you can, Princess. But a ghost cannot unlock a door, however much I'd like to help you." Sir Galahad plunged his arm through the wood to demonstrate.

Rhianna frowned. "You steered the ship that brought us here," she pointed out.

"That's different. The Grail ship is enchanted and will only respond to the hands of the dead. The Fisher King made it that way to stop power-hungry living people, like your Prince Mordred, from using it to find this castle and the Light the maidens guard here."

She sighed. "Then go and find someone living to unlock it for us," she said.

"In this castle, the living sleep by day," Sir Galahad explained. "I'm afraid you'll have to wait until evening."

"Oh, for goodness' sake!" Rhianna clenched her fists. "What sort of a ghost are you? Can't you wake someone *up?*"

"The living do not normally see ghosts, unless they are in the presence of one of the Lights." Sir Galahad reminded her.

His gaze rested on Arianrhod, clutching her bulging pack, and Rhianna's heart thumped. Did he guess what was inside?

"That's no problem," she said quickly. "My champion Cai still has the Lance of Truth." She hoped so, anyway. "He'll hear you. Send him up here – I bet he knows a way to open a locked door. Then go and get the ship ready to sail. We might need to leave in a hurry."

"As you wish, Princess." Sir Galahad gave her another strange look before rippling back through the door.

Rhianna lifted her hand from Excalibur and sighed. Controlling the ghost had taken what was left of her energy. The bed with its damp covers suddenly seemed very inviting. She sat on the edge of it with the sword resting across her knees.

While they waited, she began to polish the blade. Maybe she should have used the sword's magic to summon Sir Bors' spirit instead?

Would that have woken the big knight from his enchanted sleep, or just brought his dreaming spirit out of his body? She could not think straight. Excalibur's white jewel, shining with the magic of the castle, made her dizzy. She might try calling Sir Bors when she felt a bit stronger.

"What if Cai and Sir Bors are locked in too, my lady?" Arianrhod asked, rousing Rhianna from her thoughts.

She shook herself and laid the sword aside. "Then we'll use the window," she decided. "We're not staying in this castle another night. We've got to rescue Elphin and take the four Lights to Avalon before Mordred gets hold of them! We can escape while everyone's asleep. Help me get the sheets off the bed and those tapestries off the wall. Then if Cai doesn't come, we can knot them together and climb down."

Arianrhod looked doubtful, but did what she was told. Rhianna used Excalibur to cut the material into strips, while Arianrhod knotted the strips together to make a long, knobbly rope. The maid seemed reluctant to destroy the beautiful tapestries with their pictures of fish-people and sea horses. But when Rhianna pointed out that there would be further to fall if she didn't, she kept working.

When they'd used all the tapestries and there was still no sign of Cai, Rhianna tied one end of their makeshift rope to the bed. She threw the other end out of the window, where it disappeared into the mist.

Arianrhod looked out and paled. "I don't think I can climb all the way down there, my lady," she whispered.

"Nonsense!" Rhianna picked up their packs. "It's easy if you can't see the drop. I'll help you."

Arianrhod shook her head, tears springing to her eyes. "No, Rhia, please. You go! Take the packs with you. I'll stay here and untie the rope, say you made me help you escape. You can get away on Alba. The Fisher King won't hurt me if I'm the daughter of a Grail maiden. I'll stay here and find my mother. She'll look after me." She gave Rhianna a brave smile.

Rhianna looked at the pack with the Grail inside. It was tempting. But she'd already left Arianrhod behind once, when the maid had been locked in a cell at Camelot. That time, her friend had bravely hidden her father's Crown jewel from Mordred by swallowing it.

"No," she said firmly. "Not this time. We're going together, or not at all. They'll never forgive you for letting me take their fourth Light."

Arianrhod looked at her pack and gave a nervous giggle. "You don't really think that old cup is the Grail of Stars, do you Rhia?"

"We're going to find out," Rhianna said.

"You're going to be in a lot of trouble, you mean!" said a voice in her ear.

She spun round in alarm to see Gareth's ghost standing at her shoulder, peering out of the window too. "There are easier ways to die," the squire remarked as the door crashed open.

Rhianna drew Excalibur and thrust Arianrhod behind her. At first she could see nothing but a blinding light. Then she recognised the plump figure standing in the doorway with the Lance of Truth shining in his hand.

"Cai!" she said, lowering her blade. "Don't

burst in on us like that! I might have killed you."

"Did you want this door opened or not?" Cai said, grinning at them. He raised the Lance and blew on the glittering point. "Rubbish locks they have in this place."

"Cai!" Arianrhod ducked past Rhianna and threw herself at the surprised boy, hugging him in relief. "Thank you!"

Cai's grin widened as he looked over Arianrhod's head at the knotted tapestries. "Planning to escape out the window, were you? Do you have any idea how far down it is?"

"I don't want to know," Arianrhod said with a shudder. Seeing Gareth's ghost smirking at them, she stepped away from Cai and hid her blush behind her hair.

"Where's Sir Bors?" Rhianna asked, peering

out into the corridor. Two of the grey-cloaked guardians slumped against the wall outside, snoring gently.

"Dead to the world," Cai said. "I couldn't wake him. Them girl-guardians are all over the place, asleep too. I'm glad I'm not the only one awake. This place is really spooky, with only the ghosts to talk to."

"Watch your tongue," Gareth said. "I didn't have to show you all the way up here."

"I didn't mean you," Cai said. "I keep forgetting you're dead."

"I'd be asleep too otherwise, wouldn't I?" Gareth sighed. "Not creeping around the castle helping you steal something that could destroy us all."

"Don't be silly," Arianrhod said, picking up her pack and glancing at Rhianna. "It's probably just an old cup. And if it does turn out to be the Grail of Stars, Rhianna knows how to use it... don't you, Lady Rhia?"

Rhianna hoped someone would tell her how to use the Grail once they got to Avalon, but there was no time to worry about that now. She looked out of the window. Dusk was already falling. "We'd better hurry if we're going to get down to the ship before everyone wakes up," she said.

She picked up the guardians' bows and eased the quivers off their shoulders. She passed one weapon to Arianrhod and dropped the other out of the window.

"But I can't shoot," Arianrhod protested.

"Doesn't matter. If anybody tries to stop you, take this arrow, put it on the string and point it at them. Cai, show us where you left Sir Bors."

They hurried down a winding stair that seemed to go on forever. As they descended, Rhianna was glad they had not used the window – the knotted tapestries would not have been nearly long enough. It grew darker with every step, but Excalibur and the Lance lit their way. This was both good and bad. The Lights would also betray their escape to anybody who was awake to see them.

"Faster!" she urged.

From the narrow windows there was still enough light to show them a beautiful terraced garden with a series of ponds linked by waterfalls leading down to the sea. At the bottom, white steps glowing in the dusk led through an arch to the harbour, where she could see the ship that had brought them here.

But the first stars reflected in the pools,

and the guardians were waking up all over the castle. Several grey-cloaked figures ran to block the stairs below, arrows on their bowstrings.

"What are you doing out of bed, Princess Rhianna?" one called, frowning at her sword. "Queen Nimue said you were to stay in your room until she returns. You failed the test of the Grail so you can't go home yet."

Cai stepped in front of Rhianna and lowered the Lance. "She's not drinking any more of your potions!" he said. "We're leaving now. Let us through."

The guardians glanced at one another. They didn't seem to know what to do.

"She's not even meant to be awake…" they whispered. "The other questing knights slept for many days. We should ask Queen Nimue, but she's gone swimming…"

Outside, Gareth shouted and waved his ghostly arms. At first Rhianna couldn't think what he was doing. From the window, she saw more of the grey-cloaked guardians running across the moonlit lawn with drawn bows.

Then Cai pointed. "Damsel Rhianna, look – the mist horses!"

Rhianna leaned out of a window to see Alba and Evenstar prancing across the grass. The horses' silver coats shone in the moonlight. Their necks were arched, and their tails plumed high over their backs. They looked beautiful and magical. They also made perfect targets.

"Be careful, Alba!" she warned.

The guardians outside loosed their arrows at the two Avalonian horses. She shut her eyes in horror. When she opened them, Alba was galloping one way and Evenstar the other, their tails high, whinnying in amusement. Arrows shivered in the grass where they had misted out of range.

The grey-cloaks are stupid, Alba said. *They aim where we are not.*

Rhianna grinned. The mist horses were doing a good job of distracting the guardians in the garden, but that still left the ones at the bottom of the stair. Gareth had vanished somewhere. She looked back for Arianrhod. "Stay close," she whispered. "They can't shoot around corners. We should be all right until we get outside."

She drew a deep breath, raised Excalibur and leaped around the final corner. She found herself face to face with a stout woman in a blue dress embroidered with tiny fish like the king's cloak. The lady had dark hair streaked with silver and crinkles at the corners of her eyes. She stood unarmed in the doorway. The guardians waited warily behind her.

"Don't kill me, Princess," she said, stepping back with her hands raised. "I'm Lady Elaine. Galahad told me you might need a bit of help."

While they stared at her, Lady Elaine turned and said something to the guardians, who cast Rhianna and her friends a final glare before running off across the lawn.

"I've sent them to find Queen Nimue," Elaine explained. "That should keep them occupied for a bit, since our fish-queen is rarely found when she wants to be with her people." She smiled. "I wouldn't hang around, though. The castle is waking up, and the others will tire of their mist horse hunt soon enough."

Rhianna warily lowered her blade. "You're

Sir Galahad's mother, aren't you?" she said. "Is that why you're helping us?"

Elaine nodded and looked fondly at Arianrhod. "Among other reasons."

Arianrhod's eyes went wide. "Are you my mother, too?" she whispered.

Lady Elaine smiled. "So you guessed, did you? Yes, you were born the year Lancelot returned to Camelot with our son. He didn't realise I was pregnant again, or he might have stayed. I wish we had more time, but I can't answer questions now. Galahad will explain – he's waiting down on the ship with your drowned squire. *Go*, while you still can."

While Elaine gave Arianrhod a quick cuddle, Rhianna turned to Cai. "Where's Sir Bors?"

"That way." Cai stopped gawping at Lady

Elaine long enough to point along the shadowy corridor. "But he's a heavy lump, Damsel Rhianna. I dunno how we're going to carry him all the way down to the ship. It was bad enough getting him on his horse in the Saxon camp that time after Mordred's bloodbeards tortured him. Do you think Alba can carry him?"

"Who are you calling a lump?" growled a voice from the shadows. "There's a lot of things I'd do for you, Rhianna Pendragon, but riding your tricksy fairy horse is not one of them."

"Sir Bors!" Cai said, his face lighting up. "You're awake!"

"Not my fault if that mead last night was strong enough to knock out a horse," the big knight grumbled. "Must've slept the whole day, and my head's still pounding loud enough to wake the dead. Speaking of which, is that

Lancelot's lovely wife I see over there? How are you, Elaine my dear? Lancelot tried to come with us too, but Damsel Rhianna here had other ideas."

Lady Elaine let Arianrhod go and exchanged a few quiet words with the knight. Rhianna stared uncertainly at Sir Bors, afraid he'd become a ghost like Galahad and Gareth and the others. But then he staggered up to them and clasped her in another of his crushing hugs.

"Now what's all this I hear about leaving?" he grunted, eyeing the bulge in Arianrhod's pack. "Lady Nimue give you the Grail after she tried to poison you with it, did she?"

"Not exactly." Rhianna exchanged a glance with Arianrhod and grinned. She tossed her pack to Sir Bors. "Here – carry this.

Galahad's waiting for us on the ship. I'll explain on the way."

They ran down through the garden towards the harbour, darting from bush to bush so the guardians hunting the mist horses would not see them. Rhianna kept Excalibur in its scabbard so that the shining blade would not give them away, and Cai wrapped some leaves around the glittering head of the Lance. Arianrhod kept casting glances back at Lady Elaine, who stood in the castle doorway clutching her cloak around her shoulders.

"Did you know she was my mother?" she asked Sir Bors, but the big knight only grunted and hurried them on.

The night shadows helped hide them, and Rhianna thought they were going to make it. But as they passed the last pool, the moon rose and glinted off her armour, and a furious shout went up from the castle.

"Stop them! They've stolen Queen Nimue's cup!"

The surface of the pool rippled, and a large fish-tail splashed. Rhianna saw a swirl of green hair in the water. The guardians abandoned their mist horse hunt and came running back across the moonlit lawn, fitting new arrows to their bowstrings.

"Stay away from the pool!" Rhianna warned, drawing Excalibur and taking a stand at the top of the steps that led down to the harbour. "Quick, get on the ship – I'll hold them off."

"You'll do no such thing," Sir Bors growled, dumping their packs on the steps so he could draw his sword too.

Rhianna scowled at him. "I'll catch you up on Alba," she said. "I'm wearing my Avalonian armour so arrows can't hurt me, but they can kill you! Get Arianrhod and the packs to the ship, and cast off. That's an *order*."

Though it made her dizzy, she gripped Excalibur's jewel and concentrated on controlling the big knight's spirit.

Sir Bors glared at her. But when the first arrows hissed around Rhianna, and she still did not move her hand from Excalibur, he shook his head in annoyance. He ducked another volley of arrows, grabbed the packs in one hand and Arianrhod's wrist in the other, and hurried down the steps.

"You too, Cai," Rhianna said, gritting her teeth with the effort of using Excalibur's magic on her friends.

"I'll get the mist horses!" Cai called as he ran after the others.

Rhianna saw Sir Bors reach the harbour and toss their packs containing the Grail and the Crown on deck. She relaxed slightly and turned to face the guardians, Excalibur shining in the night. The grey-cloaked girls slithered to a stop and reached for more arrows.

"We can't let you take Queen Nimue's cup, Princess," said the one who had stood guard while Rhianna and Arianrhod bathed. "Let us pass!"

"No," Rhianna said, widening her stance as Sir Bors had taught her and bending her knees slightly. She hoped they would not try to shoot her in the legs. "My friends and I are leaving now. Don't try to stop us."

A second tail splashed in the pool, and her vision sparkled as water showered around her. She blinked the drops from her eyes and tightened her grip on her sword.

"We can't let you go home until you've completed the test of the Grail and answered Lady Nimue's riddle," the guardian said.

Rhianna smiled. "That's easy! I know the answer now."

The guardian frowned at her. "You do?" The others lowered their bows in surprise.

"Yes." Rhianna grinned. "But I'm only telling it to Lady Nimue... have you found your queen yet?" She kept a wary eye on the water and checked to see if her friends were safely on board the ship.

The guardians drew together in a huddle of grey cloaks and held a whispered discussion.

One of them knelt to speak to the fish-people in the pool.

Rhianna took the opportunity to call Alba. With a whinny and thud of hooves, her mist horse appeared right in the middle of the group. The guardians scattered in alarm, swinging their bows around to take aim at the little horse that had sprung out of nowhere.

Grey-cloaks not catch me! Alba said. *We go home now?*

"Yes, my darling!" Rhianna grabbed hold of the mane to vault into Alba's saddle, but to do this she had to lower Excalibur. A guardian grabbed her braid from behind, and Alba misted again to avoid another who tried to catch her reins. Rhianna missed the saddle and stumbled, while the mare fled across the nearby pool.

"Not that way, Alba!" she warned, in sudden

fear for her horse.

Too late. A webbed hand reached up out of the pool and seized the mare's dangling reins. Alba tried to mist again, but just blurred on the spot. The little horse snorted in fear as the fish-people dragged her head down towards the water. Her enchanted horseshoes scrabbled at the surface, and her legs splayed as she tried to escape.

Need help! she called urgently.

Rhianna swung Excalibur at the guardians to clear them out of her way and skidded to a halt at the edge of the pool. She eyed the water. How deep was it? Could she swim wearing her armour, sword and boots?

She had no choice. She dared not remove her armour, or the guardians' arrows might kill her.

"Let my horse go!" she shouted at the fish people.

She recognised two of them from the feast, younger than Lady Nimue with shells plaited into their green hair. They giggled as they dragged her poor mare further out across the water. "We've caught an Avalonian horse!" they teased. "It has very pretty shoes. Can we take them off?"

Their webbed hands reached for Alba's hooves, making the little mare squeal in fright.

Rhianna took a deep breath. She was about to dive into the pool, armour and all, when she heard a shout and another squeal behind her.

Evenstar leaped past her with Cai clinging to his mane and swinging the Lance of Truth. "Stay there, Damsel Rhianna!" he called. "I'll rescue your horse."

She blinked at him in relief. Elphin's horse must have remembered how Cai rode him last year, when they had galloped across Mordred's flood to reach Camelot. She should have been angry the boy had ignored her order to get aboard the ship. But she was glad she did not have to fight the grey-cloaked guardians alone.

Cai yelled a battle cry loud enough to frighten a dragon and lowered his Lance at the fish-girls. They let go of Alba and dived in alarm. Their tails disappeared in a sparkle of stars, and Alba immediately misted and reappeared on the bank beside Rhianna.

Hurry, the mare said, shaking her wet mane. *We go before fish-queen come.*

Rhianna did not need telling twice. She vaulted into Alba's saddle, glanced back to make sure Cai was following, and headed the mare down the steps towards the harbour at a reckless speed. Evenstar came down after her more slowly so that Cai would not fall off. The guardians' arrows rattled uselessly after them.

Only when she and Cai were safely out of reach did Rhianna risk a look back. Grey-cloaked guardians lined the quay, staring in frustration after the disappearing ship. She halted Alba and waved Excalibur in the moonlight to catch their attention.

"The Grail doesn't contain anything!" she shouted. "It's a trick question. I drank whatever was in it, and now I'm taking it to Avalon to wake my father. Tell your queen *that* when you see her!"

Grinning with triumph, she sent Alba galloping across the waves to catch up with her friends.

8

The Return

Through the mist four Lights did gleam
When our damsel had a ghostly dream,
While across the sea a harp played long
To call her prince with its broken song.

As they left the Grail Castle behind, Rhianna kept expecting Lady Nimue to surface and challenge her with yet another riddle. Alba remained nervous too, snorting at every ripple. But when the mists closed around them, making Rhianna dizzy again, she sheathed her sword. The last thing she wanted to do was drop Excalibur out here in the enchanted sea.

She trotted Alba alongside the ship, where Cai hung over the rail with a big grin on his face.

"That was fun!" he shouted. "I almost fell off, galloping down all them steps! But Evenstar's really sure-footed. D'you think Lord Avallach will let me have a mist horse of my own when we get to Avalon?"

Tell the human boy no, Alba said, with a disgusted snort.

"I'll ask him," Rhianna promised the squire with a smile. "Give me a hand, will you? I'm still feeling a bit dizzy from whatever Nimue gave me to drink last night."

Cai helped her over the rail, where she

staggered with the roll of the ship. At once Arianrhod began to fuss over her. She let the maid spread a cloak on the deck for her, and sat gratefully against the mast while Arianrhod dug into her pack for herbs and ordered Cai to fetch water. Rhianna closed her eyes with a sigh and let their voices wash over her. Now that the excitement was over, she felt very sleepy.

She kept thinking of the potion she'd drunk from Nimue's cup. *I drank it.* What if she really had been poisoned, like her friends thought?

"Do not worry, daughter. I'll look after you if you die."

With an effort, she opened her eyes. King Arthur's ghost knelt beside her on the deck, his hair blowing across his eyes.

He smiled at Rhianna and pushed one

of her braids back behind her ear. "*I've been talking to young Gareth. He tells me you accepted the challenge of the Grail and drank Lady Nimue's potion. That was a very brave thing to do, but you shouldn't have done it for me.*"

"Father!" Rhianna said, turning warm inside. "You're back!"

"*Do you think I would abandon my only daughter?*" The ghost's fingers touched her cheek. They felt warm and strong, like the fingers of the living. "*I'm sorry I had to leave you on your own in the Grail Castle. I refused Nimue's challenge when I was alive. A king has responsibilities to his people and can't undertake such quests himself however much he'd like to. I expect that's why they wouldn't let me in even now I'm dead.*"

He gave her a wry smile.

"But you're not dead! Your body's healing in Avalon, and everything's going to be all right now, because I've got the Grail of Stars! I think so, anyway…" She struggled to sit up, eager to show him the cup in Arianrhod's pack.

King Arthur's hand pushed her back down. *"No, daughter, you need to rest."*

"I haven't time to rest," Rhianna said, trying to hold on to his ghostly fingers. "I've still got to rescue Elphin and get the four Lights to Avalon! Stay with me this time, please…"

But her father's hand slipped out of her grasp. Rhianna sat up, blinked away the stars and looked quickly across the deck. Sir Bors stood near the rail with Cai, examining the Lance of Truth. Sir Galahad had taken the tiller again and was showing Gareth how to steer the ship. When Rhianna sat up, they all stopped what they were doing and smiled at her in relief.

"Where did he go?" she called. "Did you see King Arthur just now?"

Sir Galahad shook his head sadly. "Your father does not belong on this ship, Princess. He never undertook a Grail Quest."

"He was here just now!" Rhianna insisted. "Besides, Gareth's here, and he never went on a Grail Quest."

"I'm on one now, aren't I?" Gareth muttered.

"Poor girl must be running a fever..." Sir Bors began. Then King Arthur's ghost glimmered into view behind the big knight. Warmth returned to Rhianna's limbs. Sir Bors looked round and stiffened. "My king!" he said.

Galahad stopped lounging at the tiller and went down on one knee. Gareth grinned.

Cai gripped his lance and straightened his shoulders.

"It seems my daughter has done better in the Grail Castle than all of my knights put together," King Arthur said, turning his blue gaze on them all. "I thank you for helping her on her quest. Rhianna has carried Excalibur well. Are the other Lights safe?"

Arianrhod nodded. "Yes, sire. Cai over there's got the Lance of Truth. The Crown's still in my pack, and the, er... Grail's here." She lowered her gaze. "I'm afraid I dented it, I'm sorry."

"The four Lights together at last!" King Arthur's ghost touched the cup in wonder and raised Galahad. "Can this ship sail to Avalon?"

"Yes, sire," Galahad said. "But there's dark

magic guarding the gate, and I do not know the way through the mists."

The king sighed. "Then you need to find Merlin's pathfinder. I shall wait for you at the Lonely Tor. Be strong, my daughter." He faded from view.

They glanced at one another. "We'd better hope Elphin's still got the druid charm, then," Gareth muttered.

Sir Bors looked at the dented cup and guffawed. "If that thing's the Grail of Stars, then *I'm* King of Camelot! But at least we escaped with our lives, which is more than some did. And King Arthur's soul is still around so we must be doing something right. Go back to sleep, Damsel Rhianna. We'll wake you when we get back to the land of men, never fear. Then maybe we can find Lancelot and the others, and work out what to do next."

※

Rhianna lay down and pulled her cloak over her head, but she couldn't sleep. If they had the four Lights, and her father's soul was waiting for her at the gateway to Avalon, then she'd almost completed her quest. But they still had to find Elphin, and Sir Galahad seemed very nervous, for a ghost. When Sir Bors and Cai went below, she heard him mutter to Gareth about the fish-people thickening the mists so they couldn't find their way back.

"Seems we're lost," Gareth grumbled, drifting over to Rhianna. "Told you we'd be in trouble if you took the fish-queen's cup, didn't I? So what are you going to do next? The Lights don't work so good in the mist between worlds, do they?"

Rhianna pulled a face at him. "We've got other magic." Remembering how they had found Cai and the others, she threw off her cloak and hurried to the stern. "Alba," she called. "Evenstar!"

The two mist horses appeared at once, snorting in the spray behind the ship.

Rhianna leaned over the rail and untied Elphin's harp from Evenstar's saddle. She wiped off the salt and fingered the broken string.

Gareth watched her curiously. Arianrhod dozed on the deck, the stolen bow in her hand and her head resting on the quiver. The girl looked exhausted, but more determined than before. According to Galahad, who had been delighted to learn she was his little sister, Arianrhod had been sent to Camelot as a baby because her mother didn't want her growing up as a Grail maiden, unable to find love. Had Lady Elaine known that one day her daughter would be the Grail's sole guardian on its way to Avalon? Could she even have planned it from the start?

Rhianna shook the thought away and rested the harp on her knee. It felt fragile, like an Avalonian's bones. "Ask Evenstar if he can hear Elphin yet," she told Alba.

Evenstar say he hear wings, the mare reported.

Rhianna frowned up into the mist. She couldn't hear anything, but it seemed to be getting lighter. Was that a green glimmer ahead, like the enchantments they had seen around the Lonely Tor?

She ran her fingers over the strings, avoiding the broken one. The harp wailed. Gareth put his hands over his ears and grimaced. Alba and

Evenstar cantered off into the mist, shaking their heads.

Rhianna set her jaw and tried again. She might not have six fingers like an Avalonian, but it didn't matter how terrible the music sounded. If Elphin heard, he'd know they were looking for him and would use Merlin's pathfinder to open the mists for them.

"Where are you, Elphin?" she whispered, playing a bit louder. "If you can hear this, send me a sign."

Encouraged by the glimmering mist, she forgot to avoid the broken string. The harp shrieked in protest. Arianrhod jumped to her feet, bow in hand, and stared around wild-eyed. Feet pounded up the ladder, and Sir Bors stumbled out on deck with Cai at his heels. The ghosts faded from view.

Sir Bors shook his head at the harp. "What are you trying to do, Damsel Rhianna? Wake the dead?"

"You're no bard, my lady," said Arianrhod, trying not to giggle. "That's even worse than Cai played it."

"A string's broken, and it's out of tune after getting splashed with seawater," Rhianna said with a scowl. "What do you expect? Elphin should recognise its music, though, if he can hear it. Here, you try." She thrust the harp at Arianrhod. "Keep playing. I'm going to ride Alba again now it's getting lighter."

Arianrhod reluctantly took the harp. Before she could touch the strings, the Lance of Truth gleamed brightly in Cai's hand. A shadow passed across the deck and they heard the flap of wings in the mist.

Sir Bors drew his sword. "Dragon!" he warned. "Get below—"

Everyone ducked as something zipped past Rhianna's ear to land on the deck.

Rhianna snatched out Excalibur, her heart thumping. The Sword's blade glittered bright green. Cai swung the Lance around wildly, looking for the dragon. Sir Bors ran to the rail and peered into the mist. Arianrhod crouched beside the mast with her bow and the harp.

"Alba!" Rhianna called in sudden fear for her horse. "Evenstar?"

We are safe, came the mare's faint whinny.

Rhianna looked to see what had nearly hit her. An arrow, she thought at first, waving Arianrhod to stay back. Then her heart steadied as a small, bedraggled falcon hopped across the deck and fluttered up to perch on the rail.

The bird eyed Excalibur blazing in Rhianna's hand, the Lance gleaming in Cai's grasp, and Sir Bors' big sword that had nearly taken off its head. It shook itself dry and said grumpily, "Fine sort of welcome, I must say! What *are* you up to, Rhianna Pendragon? All the dead in Annwn must have been able to hear that racket."

Rhianna tightened her grip on Excalibur. "Merlin!" she said, her relief fading a little as she remembered what Nimue had told them about the druid.

Everyone crowded around the merlin, which sat on Rhianna's wrist preening its tattered feathers. It had lost a few, and others were singed as if the bird had flown through a fire. Just as well she'd pulled down the sleeve of her Avalonian armour, because the little falcon's talons gripped fiercely.

"Ask him if he's seen Lancelot and the others," Sir Bors said.

"Ask him if he knew Lady Elaine was my mother," Arianrhod whispered.

"Ask him why the fish-lady tried to poison you at the Grail Castle!" Cai interrupted.

Rhianna waved her hand to shut them up. She could hardly think with everyone shouting at once. She had plenty of questions of her own – such as, did Merlin know he was Mordred's father, and if so why hadn't he told them?

But important things first.

"Where's Elphin?" she asked, resting a hand on Excalibur's hilt so she would be able to hear the druid's reply.

Merlin finally finished preening. He put his head on one side and considered her from a pale blue eye. "The Avalonian prince is on the Lonely Tor."

Rhianna breathed again. So Elphin had made it to the Lonely Tor before he fell off. Then the magic that had stopped her using the Crown to find him must have been because they were sailing through the enchanted mists, unless...

"Is he still alive?"

"Of course he's alive." The merlin gave her a grumpy look. "Avalonians don't die that easily, you know that."

"But what *happened*, Merlin? Evenstar told Alba he'd been chased by a dragon! It was you we saw up at Nimue's lake when the mists opened, wasn't it? Is Elphin safe?"

"Safe enough when I left him," Merlin said. "Don't worry, he'll be fine until I get back."

Rhianna relaxed slightly. "What about Mordred's bloodbeards?" she asked, glancing at Gareth. "Did you see any of them on the Tor? Is Mordred's ghost over there, too?"

The druid gave her a sharp look. "Whoever gave you that idea?"

"Me," Gareth interrupted. "I saw the traitor when his bloodbeards drowned me... and he had both his hands, too!"

Merlin sighed. "Squire Gareth's still telling tales, I see. Don't do anything stupid, Rhianna Pendragon. Your Avalonian friend will understand your quest comes first. We must work quickly now if we're going to bring King Arthur back. I hear you've been to the Grail Castle – did you find what you were looking for?"

Remembering her father's body lying

in the crystal caverns, Rhianna took a deep breath. "Yes… at least, I think so. Show him, Arianrhod." The maid pulled Nimue's cup from her pack. It looked quite ordinary again, dull and dented. "Do you know what the Grail of Stars looks like, Merlin? Is this it?"

The druid went very still. He eyed the cup warily. Then he fluffed his feathers and said, "Don't ask me, Rhianna Pendragon. None of Arthur's knights succeeded in bringing the Grail back to Camelot. There's only one way to find out for sure if you've got the fourth Light."

"What's that?" She gave him a suspicious look. Did he mean she had to drink from the cup again?

"Take it to Avalon and see if it works, of course!" Merlin snapped. "I've just got a small problem to sort out over on the Tor. Then I'll be back to help you open the spiral path."

Rhianna set her jaw. "I'm not going anywhere without Elphin! Did he hurt himself when he fell off, is that it? Because if he did, we need to get him into Lord Avallach's crystal caverns as soon as possible so he can be healed. We can easily take this ship across and pick him up on our way. Show us where you left him." She lifted her wrist so the merlin could take off more easily.

"I'm afraid that's impossible," Merlin said, twisting his head to scan the sky. "You're right, there *are* bloodbeards on the Lonely Tor, which is why you mustn't go over there. It's a trap. Take your ship into the marshes and wait for me there. You'd better hurry – I think I've been followed."

"It won't make any difference where we

hide if Mordred knows we're here," Gareth's ghost whispered in her ear. "Ask him again if he saw the dark knight on the Tor. He never answered you last time."

Rhianna frowned at the interruption. But the squire had been right about the bloodbeards who drowned him.

"Is Mordred's ghost on the Tor?" she asked again, a little chill going down her back.

The druid did not answer.

"Merlin!" she said, giving her wrist a shake. "I know all about you and Morgan Le Fay. Lady Nimue told me. She said Mordred's your son… is that why you don't want me to go over to the Tor, in case I find out you're his father? Because I don't care about that. If Elphin's in danger, we've got to rescue him as soon as possible. Take me to him, quick!"

Merlin's talons gripped tighter. "No, Rhianna. I can't."

She scowled at the bird, getting suspicious now. "Can't or won't?" she said, beginning to suspect there was something else he was not telling them.

Just then a shadow fell across the deck, and they heard large wing beats overhead. The merlin fluttered to the rail. "Why can't you ever make anything easy, Rhianna Pendragon?" it grumbled. "I told you I'd been followed. Now we're all in trouble."

Alba whinnied faintly. *I am frightened. Evenstar lost his rider near here.*

The shadow took on the shape of a dragon. Across the water, a warrior on a ghostly green horse rode out of the mist, raised his axe and shook it at them.

"It's Uther Pendragon's ghost!" Gareth warned.

Rhianna's blood ran cold, and suddenly she knew what Merlin was so reluctant to tell them – if Uther's ghosts could ride out of Annwn, then Mordred could ride with them.

"Alba!" she called, running to the rail. "Alba! I need you now!"

As she hooked her leg over the rail to mount her mare, the merlin flew at her, flapping its wings in her face and screeching. "Stop, foolish girl! Are you trying to get yourself killed?"

"I'm doing what you can't do! Hide here on the ship, if you want. *I'm* not afraid of the ghosts of Annwn!" She clenched her fist, ready to knock the merlin out of the air, if she had to.

"I'm not afraid of them, either!" Cai said, ducking under Sir Bors' arm and running to the rail after her. "Get Alba to call Evenstar, Damsel Rhia. I'll ride him like I did before, and send Mordred's ghost back to Annwn for you."

"Please don't go, Rhia!" Arianrhod begged. "What if someone tries to steal the Crown or the Grail while you're away?"

Rhianna hesitated. "Sir Bors will look after you. So will Sir Galahad – I bet he can fight Uther's ghosts." The golden-haired knight grinned and nodded.

"It's not ghosts you should be worrying about," Gareth muttered, but in all the excitement nobody took any notice of the dead squire.

Alba and Evenstar galloped up to the rail, snorting and shaking their manes. *Are we going home now?* her mare asked.

"Soon, my darling," Rhianna promised. "We've just got to rescue Elphin first."

Cai was already scrambling clumsily over the rail and into Evenstar's saddle. The Lance got trapped between the ship and his leg, and Rhianna held her breath as the second Light began to slide into the water.

Sir Bors reached over and caught the Lance, passing it to Cai with a sigh. "Don't go getting yourself killed, lad," he muttered. "Stay on your horse at all times. Don't accept any duels. And if you find yourself fightin' more than three of the enemy at once, ghosts or not, forget about knightly code and *run*. Got it?"

Cai grinned. "Yes sir!"

"That goes for you too, Damsel Rhianna," Sir Bors said.

Rhianna smiled grimly. "Merlin," she warned, gripping Excalibur. "We're going to the Tor now to find Elphin. I'm not leaving him here. I don't care if you came to help us like you say, or if you're working with Mordred's witch-mother like Lady Nimue thinks you are – but if you try to stop me I'll knock your bird body unconscious."

The merlin hopped back to the rail. "Wait!" the druid said. "Before you go over there, you should know Mordred isn't—" But a huge black dragon dived out of the mist, drowning out the druid's words with its deafening roar.

"WE MEET AGAIN, PENDRAGON MAID."

Rhianna drew Excalibur and swung her blade at the shadrake as a huge wingtip tore down their sails. Its talons thumped into the rail where the merlin had perched only moments before. Feathers spiralled into the water as the druid took off. He left half his tail under the shadrake's claw, but made it to the top of the mast, screeching.

Rhianna couldn't hear a word in all the chaos. She swung her sword at the shadrake again, and yelled at Cai to get the mist horses away from the ship. Sir Bors pushed Arianrhod flat on the deck, covering her with his body. Sir Galahad and Gareth, being ghosts, simply faded out of sight.

The cup was shining again, as it had done at the feast. Rhianna's breath caught as the bright silver light spilled out between Arianrhod's fingers. The shadrake's head turned and it breathed a plume of ice across the deck, frosting the ropes. Alba misted in alarm. Evenstar nearly misted after the mare, but Cai shouted something, and the little horse reappeared beneath the boy before he fell into the water.

"Did you lead the shadrake here?" Rhianna yelled at Merlin, furious that she'd trusted him.

The druid's reply was lost in another shriek from the shadrake as it dived after Alba.

HELP! her mist horse called.

Cai bravely rode Evenstar into the dragon's path and aimed the Lance of Truth at its belly. The Lance glittered with magic, but the shadrake showed no sign of pulling up.

"Cai!" Rhianna yelled. "Get out of its way, you idiot! You're riding on water, remember. It'll freeze you to the spot if you stay still... *ride!*"

She had both legs over the rail now, ready to jump into her saddle. But Alba was too afraid to approach the ship with the shadrake diving overhead.

A harp tinkled in the mist, distracting the

shadrake from its prey. Evenstar's ears flicked forward. Relief shivered across Rhianna's neck as she looked round for Elphin. But, of course, it wasn't the prince playing. Arianrhod had put the Grail between her feet so she could pluck the Avalonian harp. Sir Bors stood guard over her, his sword raised to keep the shadrake away.

The notes sounded a lot sweeter than when Rhianna had tried to play earlier. But Arianrhod had only five fingers on each hand, not six like Elphin, and a string was broken. Instead of making the shadrake sleepy, the music drew its attention. The creature abandoned its attack on the mist horses and swooped across the deck towards Sir Bors and the girl, knocking down the mast with its tail on the way. The broken string twanged as Arianrhod lost concentration.

"No!" Rhianna shouted at the dragon. "Leave my friend alone!"

Alba cantered up to the rail while the dragon was distracted, whinnying for her to mount. Rhianna hesitated, torn between staying to help her friends on the ship, and galloping after Cai.

"Damsel Rhia!" Cai called. "Hurry!"

Rhianna set her jaw. She slid back down on deck and leaped the fallen mast. She tugged at her pack, which had been trapped beneath. Green light spilled out of it. The merlin was screeching at her again, but she had to put down Excalibur to undo the straps, so its words made no sense. She hoped the Crown had not been damaged when the mast fell on top of it.

The shadrake, distracted by the green light, swung its head her way.

"Rhia!" Cai yelled. "Look out…"

The Crown was stuck. She gritted her teeth, braced her feet against the mast and pulled with all her strength. "Come *on*," she muttered.

Something fluttered past her cheek, and the merlin landed on her shoulder. It pecked her ear and screeched again. "Not now, Merlin, I'm busy," Rhianna muttered as the dragon's shadow fell over them. She grabbed Excalibur and swung the blade two-handed towards the diving shadrake.

"… *said* let me take care of this," the druid finished, gliding from her shoulder to perch on the fallen mast. He pecked at the wood, and the mast sparkled. The Crown of Dreams rolled clear.

Rhianna seized the third Light and jammed it on to her head. She kept Excalibur pointed at the dragon, while she closed her eyes and reached for the magical Jewel of Annwn that contained the secret of dragon riding.

With a lurch, her spirit jumped into the shadrake's body. Darkness shifted in her head, and as the dragon dived she had a sickening glimpse of herself kneeling by the fallen mast, looking very small. Her hair frizzed like fire around the Crown of Dreams.

"Shadrake!" she commanded. "I wear the Pendragon crown! I order you to stop attacking this ship and my friends."

The image of herself, kneeling on the deck with her sword raised, rushed closer. She braced herself for the collision. But just as she thought the stupid creature would impale itself and sink their ship, the dragon back-winged.

"I OBEY, PENDRAGON MAID," the creature boomed.

Its tail slammed into the deck as it pulled out of its dive. Amidst the crash of splintering wood, Rhianna's spirit jerked back into her body. She felt its talons brush harmlessly through her hair and lowered Excalibur in relief.

As the shadrake flapped away, she remembered Merlin and looked for the druid. Her heart gave an extra thud. The little falcon lay beneath the mast, its wings twisted and its neck bent at an unnatural angle.

"*Merlin!*" She dropped to her knees beside the motionless bird. The bedraggled little body was still warm, but she could not feel a heartbeat. She stared at the falcon in disbelief. The druid couldn't be dead.

She had time to hope that Elphin could remember how to use the pathfinder. Then the shadrake flapped back overhead and breathed frost into her hair.

"DO NOT LOOK FOR ME IN THAT LITTLE BODY, RHIANNA PENDRAGON. I HAVE STRONGER WINGS NOW."

She looked up. Her heart leaped in hope as she remembered how druids could transfer their spirits into different bodies when their old ones died. "Merlin…?"

"YOU WILL NOT BE NEEDING THIS CROWN ANY MORE."

Before she thought to duck, the shadrake neatly plucked the Crown of Dreams from her head and dropped it into the treasure-pouch between its forelegs. Several strands of her hair went with it.

"Ow!" she said, remembering they still didn't know if they could trust the druid. "That's my father's crown! Give it back, I order you."

The shadrake snorted. "YOU DO NOT CONTROL *MY* SPIRIT, RHIANNA PENDRAGON! I SHALL TAKE THE THIRD LIGHT TO TRADE FOR THE PATHFINDER. WHEN YOU GET TO AVALON, FILL THE GRAIL AT THE MOON POOL AND TAKE THE WATER INTO THE CRYSTAL CAVERNS FOR ARTHUR. I SHALL MEET YOU THERE. STAY AWAY FROM THE TOR. I CAN DEAL WITH MORDRED NOW I AM IN THIS BODY. DO NOT FOLLOW ME."

"Wait!" Rhianna called, determined to get a straight answer before Merlin flew off again.

"How can you deal with Mordred if he's a ghost now?"

"MORDRED IS NOT DEAD!" the shadrake boomed. "HE HAS DRUID BLOOD SO HE SURVIVED THE FIRE. YOU MUST BURN HIS DARK FIST TO FINISH HIM."

Rhianna felt sick. So the dark knight was still alive! Gareth had been right all along. Oh, why hadn't she listened to the squire's ghost, instead of charging off after the Grail and leaving Elphin in danger on the Tor?

"What about Elphin?" she demanded. "Is he hurt?"

But the shadrake had flapped off into the mist, green light trailing from its tail.

She stared after it in frustration. How far could they trust the druid?

Cai gaped after the dragon, too. Holding the Lance, of course, he must have heard every word.

"Maybe next time you'll listen to me," Gareth said, rippling back into view with his arms folded.

Arianrhod set down Elphin's harp beside the Grail and rushed over to the motionless merlin. She stroked its bedraggled feathers and let out a sob. "Oh, Rhia… I'm so sorry. Is your hawk dead?"

Rhianna nodded, distracted. "Yes."

"Poor old Merlin!" the maid said. "What happened to his spirit? Did the shadrake kill him?"

"No…" Rhianna frowned at the sky, wondering why Merlin had risked spirit riding the shadrake again. It wouldn't let the druid's spirit stay in its body very long, if she knew the creature. Did Merlin really mean to rescue Elphin and bring them the pathfinder?

"The mast must've crushed him," Sir Bors said. He shook his head at the dead bird and kicked the splintered wood. "Well, we're in a fine mess now. I don't know what Merlin was thinking of, leading that dragon here! It'll take ages to fix up those sails. We're takin' on water too by the looks of things, and God only knows where we are." He frowned into the mist. "Although… is that land I see, or just my old eyes playing up?"

Rhianna tightened her grip on Excalibur and stared across the water. Rising out of the fog, she saw a lone hill. Uther's ghosts glimmered green around its shore.

"It's the Lonely Tor!" Cai said. "We're back in the land of men."

Rhianna was still trying to decide whose side Merlin was on. His warning echoed in her head. *Do not follow me.*

She grinned at her friends. "At least we've found the missing Tor!" Before anyone could stop her, she'd climbed over the rail into Alba's saddle. "Elphin's over there. Come on, Cai. Let's go and spoil Mordred's fun."

Dark Bargain

Mordred paced up and down the chapel. Every time he passed a window, he stopped to scowl at the green mist that surrounded the Tor. It had grown thicker since Merlin left with the shadrake on his tail. He'd sent the dragon after the bird to make sure the druid came back. But they had both been gone far too long.

He turned his scowl on the Avalonian boy, who lay motionless on the altar, his wrists and ankles tightly bound with Morgan Le Fay's enchanted rope. Gareth's mother knelt beside the captive, crumbling herbs into a bowl and using a rag to drip her potion between his lips. It did no good that Mordred could see.

"If the druid's tricked me…" he growled, clenching his mortal fist until pus oozed out. "I'll wring his pathetic hawk-neck!"

The woman looked up fearfully. "I'm sure he hasn't, my lord," she whispered. "You're his son. Every parent wants to help their child." A tear trickled down her cheek as she looked at her patient, obviously thinking of her drowned boy.

"Oh, stop your snivelling, woman!" He kicked her bowl with his shadow-foot. It clanged against the wall, spilling its contents across the floor. Candle flames hissed as the chapel darkened. "You don't know *my* parents, and that shadrake's no more trustworthy than the druid. Wouldn't surprise me if the pair of them haven't flown off to Avalon and forgotten all about me."

Then he heard wing beats outside in the mist and saw a black shadow swoop towards the tower. At least his shadrake was back. With any luck, it would have killed the druid and saved him the bother.

"Leave us!" he ordered the woman. "Run down to the village and see if there's any sign of my cousin yet. I've things to do up here."

Gareth's mother flinched as the shadrake landed on the roof, knocking off some tiles. She checked the fairy prince a final time, before escaping down the path to the beach.

Mordred climbed the bell tower to reach the shadrake's level. He kept his mortal fist safely hidden under his cloak.

"Well?" he said. "Did you manage to get me any of the Lights?"

The creature's neck curved downwards. Its huge eye peered in through one of the arches at Mordred. Deliberately, it breathed ice over him.

Mordred stood his ground as the shadrake's breath frosted his hair. His shadow-body could not feel the cold.

"YES," boomed the dragon. "I HAVE GOT ONE OF THE LIGHTS."

"Good." Mordred's heart beat faster. He held out his shadow-hand. "Give it to me." Would it be the Lance or the Crown, he wondered. Probably not Excalibur, knowing his cousin – and he doubted she'd managed to find the Grail. But any Light would be of some help when the girl got here.

The shadrake's snout came closer. Mordred did not like the look in its glowing red eye.

"NOT YET," it said. "FIRST GIVE ME THE SPIRAL PATHFINDER YOU TOOK FROM THE AVALONIAN PRINCE."

Mordred frowned. He closed his mortal fist over the silver spiral hanging around his neck.

"I don't make bargains with dragons," he said. "I'm a Pendragon, remember! *You* must obey me."

"YOU DO NOT WEAR THE PENDRAGON CROWN," the shadrake pointed out, its eye whirling in amusement. "I HAVE IT IN MY POUCH. IF YOU WANT IT BACK, YOU MUST GIVE ME MY PATHFINDER."

My pathfinder? Mordred scowled. What on earth did the stupid creature mean? But at least it had brought him the Crown – now he just had to work out how to get it out of the dragon's pouch without losing the druid charm in the process.

As he looked for somewhere safe to leave the little spiral, he heard ghostly hand claps behind him. "Oh, very good Merlin!" said an amused voice. "Almost worthy of one of your old tricks."

Mordred spun round to see his mother's spirit glimmering at the top of the steps. "Having trouble with that shadrake, my son?" she continued. "It always was a wilful creature. Not to worry, though. I doubt the druid will be in control of it for very much longer."

She turned her attention back to the

dragon. "Nice try, my dear. What happened? The shadrake eat your little falcon's body? Saved our boy the trouble of wringing its neck, anyway."

"You mean…?" Mordred stared into the shadrake's red eye and saw the truth. "*Merlin!*" he whispered, taking a step backwards as he realised what must have happened. No wonder the shadrake and the merlin had been gone so long – the druid had made another spirit transfer!

"GOING TO WRING MY NECK, WERE YOU?" said the shadrake. "WITH YOUR PUNY MORTAL FIST? YOU ARE WELCOME TO TRY, *MY SON.*"

"No," Mordred said, taking another step backwards. "I didn't really mean it… *Mother!* Do something!"

The witch laughed again. "It was your idea to let the druid fly off to look for King Arthur's daughter. You're lucky he didn't take his pathfinder with him the first time – if he had, Rhianna and her friends would be in Avalon with the Grail of Stars by now, and we'd be in a lot more trouble than we are already. Don't be such a coward, my son. You no longer need to fear injury, remember. Your shadow-body cannot be harmed by man or dragon. Watch."

As she spoke, she walked fearlessly around the belfry underneath the shadrake, unwinding another length of glowing green rope from her waist. The dragon could not see what she was doing, but Mordred saw the witch loop her green rope around the dragon's hind leg and grinned. He'd forgotten his body was more or less invincible now.

He took a deep breath and stepped closer to distract the shadrake. "Did you see the Grail? Has my cousin found it?"

The creature's eye gleamed. "MAYBE."

"What do you mean, *maybe*? Don't you know? I thought you were supposed to be a druid! You ought to know such things." He clenched his fist tighter about the spiral, forgetting it was his mortal hand. One of his rotting fingers snapped off inside his gauntlet, and Mordred yelled in sudden pain.

His mother chose this moment to pull the green rope tight. "Well don't just stand there, foolish boy!" she snapped. "Tie this to something strong." She tossed the other end to Mordred, at the same time throwing a glittering spell into the shadrake's eyes.

Mordred fumbled the catch with his broken finger. But the witch's magic confused the creature long enough for him to knot the other end of her enchanted rope around a pillar. The shadrake shrieked in fury and tried to take off, but the enchanted ropes of Annwn kept it tethered. Tiles rattled around them as its huge wings crashed against the roof. Mordred retreated down the stairwell in alarm.

His mother's ghost rippled through the dragon's thrashing tail and smiled at the creature. "Even the great druid Merlin doesn't know everything… do you, my dear? Or you would never have lain with me that night, knowing our child would turn out to be such a needy fool. Mordred here had all the advantages. Raised as a prince of Camelot and knighted by King Arthur, with a powerful enchantress for a mother, the last of the druids for a father and an army of bloodbeards supplied by our allies in the North. Yet he lets a half-grown girl – a damsel who grew up in Fairyland with no knowledge of battle – get the better of him! What are we supposed to do with the boy?"

Mordred caught his breath. He hated it when his mother talked over his head like this. But he had to admit her magic came in useful at times. He hoped her rope would subdue the shadrake before the stupid thing demolished the tower.

"You brought me into this world, Mother!" he snapped. "The least you can do is help me rule it! I'll soon find out if my cousin's got the Grail. And if she has, then I'll make her give it to me. She and her friends might hold more of the Lights than we do, but *I've* got her precious fairy prince."

He glanced down the stair at his captive lying on the altar and smiled, imagining Rhianna's reaction when she saw the Avalonian boy.

"As for your bargain, Father," he continued, more confident now the shadrake couldn't reach him. "I'll keep your pathfinder – and I'll allow you to keep the Crown of Dreams for a bit longer. I'll get it out of your pouch later, when my mother's magic has stolen your dragon-strength. Besides, I want to be awake when my cousin Rhianna arrives. As you say, Mother, my cousin's a damsel. That's her weakness. She might carry her father's sword, but we'll soon see how much of a warrior she really is, when she's faced with a choice between her quest and her heart."

The shadrake hissed a final plume of ice at him. Mordred turned his back on the angry creature, walked through his mother's ghost, and headed down the stairs. He made himself walk slowly, even though his neck prickled with every step at the thought the dragon might get loose. He only hoped the druid's spirit would not escape the dragon's body.

Morgan Le Fay's ghost followed him down the tower. "Be careful, my son," she warned. "When the girl gets here, she'll try to use the Lights she holds to rescue her friend."

"That's where you come in," Mordred said. He glanced up at the rafters above the altar and smiled. "My cousin never stops to look before she leaps. We'll fix one of your enchanted nets up there in the shadows. Our brave Rhianna won't see it until too late."

9

To the Rescue

A fairy prince by enchantments bound
In darkest chapel shall be found.
Those who love Arthur must take sides
When the Wild Hunt from Avalon rides.

The two Avalonian horses galloped through the green mist towards the Lonely Tor, kicking up a silver spray. Excalibur shone in Rhianna's hand and the Lance of Truth glittered in Cai's, clearing a path through Uther's shadowy warriors.

Rhianna smiled grimly. Their mad race reminded her of last year, when she and Cai had ridden across the flood surrounding Camelot and fought their way through her grandfather Uther's ghost-army to reach Mordred. Back then the Saxons had helped them. This time, they had only Sir Bors and the two ghosts on the ship to help them… and possibly Merlin, if he was still on their side.

Mordred is alive.

She thought of the shadrake carrying off Mordred's dark fist last year, and Lady Nimue's warning to burn all of him. She had tried using the Crown of Dreams to persuade the dragon to bring the fist back again so they could burn that too, but dark magic had worked against her. Now she knew why – Mordred must have been using the fist to grow his new body.

She gripped her sword tighter. When she met her cousin this time, she'd be ready for his tricks.

"Do you think Merlin can control that shadrake?" Cai called, looking nervously at the sky.

"We'll soon find out!" Rhianna shouted back. "Stay close to me when we reach the Tor. Don't get separated. The important thing is to rescue Elphin and find Merlin's spiral pathfinder so we can get the Lights to Avalon before Mordred gets hold of them."

She slowed Alba when they reached the beach, and they trotted warily between the dark rocks. Seaweed swirled around the mare's hooves. The little horse crunched one of the pods between her teeth and snorted in surprise.

Salty apple!

"That's not an apple, silly," Rhianna said, looking for a path off the beach.

As they left the water, Evenstar pricked his ears and neighed loudly.

"Shh!" she warned. "We don't want to announce our presence to the whole Tor."

"Er... I think we've already done that," Cai said. He pointed at the cloaked figures running towards them along the beach.

Rhianna gripped Excalibur tighter, her heart thumping. But it wasn't Mordred's bloodbeards, as she'd feared. An old man in a stained monk's robe stumbled up to them and caught Alba's rein.

"Thank God you're here, Princess!" he gasped. "Prince Mordred's devils have taken over the island! They won't let anyone leave. They cast us out of our church and drowned one of your boys while he was here visiting his poor mother. The devil himself is up there, with that foul dragon and God knows what else out of Annwn..." His voice trailed off as he noticed Cai's youth. He frowned at the sword in Rhianna's hand and peered hopefully behind her. "How many men have you brought?"

Rhianna stared up at the Tor. The green mist hid its summit, but she could just make out a dark tower on top, where black wings flapped against purple lightning. She shivered, reminded of her vision when she'd worn the Crown on the day the Saxons had brought Gareth's body to Camelot.

"Have you seen Mordred, then?" she asked, shaking spray from her braids. "We thought he was dead, but I've been told he's still alive."

"Dead or alive, what's the difference when

he has dark magic on his side? There's some swear they've seen his witch-mother up there, too, and she's been dead for years." The monk scowled. "But we'll be all right now Arthur's knights are here – they'll know what to do." He cast a relieved look at their ship coming out of the mist.

Rhianna pulled a face. "It's obvious what we need to do – we've got to stop Mordred! Have you seen an Avalonian boy? Violet eyes and six fingers on each hand? He's our friend."

The others muttered uneasily. A woman pushed forward, her eyes swollen from crying. "I did my best for him, Princess," she said. "But I am afraid he's going to die, like my poor Gareth…" She glanced up at the Tor and its purple lighting.

"Elphin's in your church, isn't he?" Rhianna

headed Alba for the path that wound up the hillside.

"Wait, Princess!" called the monk, running after her. "You can't go up there."

"King Arthur's daughter can go anywhere she likes," Cai said, lowering his lance across the monk's path. "We're on Pendragon business. Stand aside!"

With a rattle of hooves, Evenstar came cantering after Alba.

"No, I mean there's dark magic at work in that tower," the monk said. "You can't go up there alone, Princess – it's too dangerous! At least wait for your knights."

Rhianna had no intention of waiting for anyone. If Elphin was Mordred's captive, then she had to rescue her friend as soon as possible. She checked Cai was still in his saddle and urged her mare into a gallop. "Race, Alba!" she whispered.

By the time they reached the top of the Tor, both mist horses were breathing hard. It was cooler up in the clouds, and thick green mist hid the path. At first she thought they had come the wrong way. Then the church loomed before them, apparently deserted. Lightning still flashed around its tower, where she could make out the dark form of the shadrake filling the belfry. But the creature was too big to enter the building, and seemed to be asleep.

Rhianna forgot about the dragon. The door stood open. Inside, she could just make out an altar with candles flickering around it. A body lay on it, unnaturally still.

"It's Elphin!" Cai said, gripping his lance with a fierce look. "Mordred's killed him!"

He tried to make Evenstar approach the door. But the little horse shook his mane and backed away, snorting with fear.

Smells bad in there, Alba warned.

Rhianna hardly heard. She leaped off the mare and ran towards the door, Excalibur blazing in her hand. Elphin's wrists and ankles had been bound with glowing green ropes. Seaweed was tangled in his dark curls and his eyes were closed.

Every nerve in her body wanted to rush inside and free him. But remembering Merlin's warning about the trap, she stopped at the doorway. The chapel smelled musty, like a dragon's lair. Her skin tingled with echoes of magic.

"He's not dead," she whispered to Cai, who had dismounted to join her. "There's no need to tie a dead person's hands and feet to stop him running away, is there?"

Cai didn't look convinced. "Is he asleep?"

"I don't know." Rhianna took a shuddering breath and warily thrust Excalibur's gleaming blade through the doorway to check the shadows inside. "I can't see anyone in there with him. Wait out here with the horses. If anything happens to me, ride straight down to the beach and fetch Sir Bors."

Cai tightened his grip on his lance. "I'm not leaving you, Damsel Rhia!"

"Guard the door, then. No sense both of us getting caught, if it is a trap."

She took a careful step inside the chapel. Then another. Nobody jumped her. When she swung Excalibur round in a circle, she couldn't see any bloodbeards lurking in the dark.

She continued slowly across the chapel to the altar. Keeping a good hold on Excalibur, she touched Elphin's cheek with her free hand. It felt like ice. The ropes seemed to be stuck to his skin and glowed brighter green when she tugged at them.

"Elphin?" she whispered. "Can you hear me?"

At the sound of her voice, a freezing wind howled through the doorway, blowing out the candles and plunging the chapel into darkness. She whirled as the heavy chapel door slammed shut behind her. She heard Cai banging on it and his voice calling faintly, "Damsel Rhianna! Are you all right in there? What happened?"

Excalibur was blazing brightly again. But she still couldn't see anyone. Her heartbeat slowed. It must have been a draught. She

opened her mouth to tell Cai she was fine –
and a chuckle came out of the shadows behind
the altar.

"I knew you would come, cousin."

Her scalp prickled. She knew that voice.

She turned slowly. A figure dressed all in
black stood at the foot of the stairs leading up
to the bell tower.

"*Mordred*," she hissed. She clenched her fist
on Excalibur and took a step towards him.

The dark knight spread his arms wide
and grinned at her, inviting her to attack. She
couldn't see a weapon under his cloak, and
they seemed to be alone in here. Fearing a
trick, Rhianna hesitated. She glanced up the
stairs. Was the shadrake still up there? It was
very quiet.

"I knew you wouldn't abandon Lord

Avallach's son," Mordred continued. "The fairy lord won't be very pleased when you return to Avalon without its prince. I doubt he'll give you back your father's body once he hears the sad news."

Fear for Elphin banished her caution. "What have you *done* to him?" She sprang around the altar and rushed at her cousin, sword raised. As she did so, Mordred looked up and smiled.

Rhianna slithered to a stop as a green glimmer fell from the rafters and landed over her head, entangling her in sticky, glowing ropes like those that bound Elphin. Just as Merlin had warned her, it was a trap and she'd walked straight into it!

Excalibur had caught in the net as it fell. But she still managed to keep hold of her sword and slashed desperately at the cords to stop them from tightening around her. The ropes recoiled under the enchanted blade, hissing with green smoke. She struggled free with a shudder and ran to the door. But she could not open it. A green curtain shimmered across it, like the one that had kept them out of the fort at the North Wall, when Mordred had been duelling with Sir Lancelot. She tried to slice her way through using Excalibur, but as fast as she cut it the curtain sealed again. From behind the green veil, Morgan Le Fay's spirit smiled at her... *dark magic.*

"Get help, Cai!" she yelled. "Mordred's in here with the witch's spirit!"

Mordred stalked her slowly across the chapel, swinging a large battleaxe he'd been hiding behind the altar.

"Still fighting, cousin?" he said with a chuckle. "Such a shame to fail your quest because you cared too much for an Avalonian boy. He's not mortal, you know. He doesn't care about you."

"That's not true!" Rhianna said thinking of the gentle kiss Elphin had given her back at Camelot when she'd been accepted as King Arthur's daughter. She ducked under the dark knight's axe and swung Excalibur towards what should have been Mordred's crippled leg. But he leaped the shining blade to land behind her.

She whirled in surprise, and he laughed at her expression.

"That was hardly fair, cousin, now was it?" he said. "What about your father's knightly code? If an opponent is crippled or wounded, you must give him a chance to surrender before you try to kill him."

She stared at his leg. It was difficult to see in the shadows, but it did not look twisted any more. He kept his right arm hidden under his cloak, though, and held his battleaxe in his left hand.

She smiled grimly. "You didn't give my father a chance to surrender before you killed him, did you?" she said. "I saw you duelling in Merlin's song-pictures. You betrayed him! Your own uncle and king."

"Betrayed is a strong word," Mordred said. "And Arthur chopped off my sword hand in that duel. So we're even."

Rhianna backed towards the altar. He came after her, swinging his axe until she was forced to grip Excalibur with both hands to ward off his blows. Her blade did not break – it had been forged in Avalon, which made it stronger than any mortal blade – but her arms trembled with effort. Her cousin felt so much stronger than the last time they had fought! And his leg definitely seemed to be healed, though he still kept his right hand hidden. She remembered Gareth's ghost claiming Mordred had two hands now, and shuddered.

All had gone silent at the door. She hoped Cai had gone to fetch the others. She tried to remember what Sir Bors had taught them in sword training if they found themselves fighting a stronger opponent. *Height and cover… use the surroundings to your advantage.* Watching for her chance, she thrust Excalibur at Mordred's right arm to make him overbalance, and then sprang the other way. If she could put the altar between them, she might be able to delay him until the knights came.

She'd forgotten the witch's net. As she leaped, the ropes coiled up from the floor and curled around her ankles. She fell flat on her face, winded. Mordred put his foot on her blade and chuckled. She tugged desperately, but the Sword would not come free. Her arm felt weak, as if she'd banged the nerve in her elbow. The strength trickled out of her.

He looked down at her and shook his head. "Can't fight magic, cousin. My mother made that net especially for me to catch annoying little flies like you and your fairy prince. It was spun in the dark by the creatures of Annwn, from lost souls eager for the memory of flesh and blood. It's strong enough to hold a dragon, so there's no point fighting. Feeling weak yet? The more you struggle, the more it will feed on your strength." He raised his axe over her wrist. "I'd advise letting go of your sword – unless you want to lose a hand like I did." He chuckled.

Rhianna stopped struggling. There was only one way to fight magic… with magic.

She shut her eyes, gripped Excalibur's hilt tighter and called on the spirits of the knights linked to the white jewel. *Come!* she commanded silently. *I need you NOW*.

Sir Bors felt near. But she also sensed Sir Bedivere not far away, and Sir Lancelot and Sir Agravaine on their way through the mist. Maybe they would arrive before Mordred killed her? She really didn't want to lose a hand. But she wasn't letting go of her sword so the dark knight could use Excalibur against her, as he had done last winter at Camelot.

With an effort she moved her other arm,

ready to catch the Sword in her right hand if Mordred carried out his threat to chop it free of her left. She saw his axe glint and braced herself for the pain. Then she heard a scrape at the door, and the axe swung away from her arm as Mordred turned.

Her breath whooshed out in relief as ghostly hands tore through the green curtain and the witch's face disappeared. Sir Galahad and his friend Sir Percival climbed through, their pale blades gleaming.

"Need some help, Princess?" Sir Galahad said.

Mordred made a frustrated sound as the ghostly knights raised their swords and rushed him. As they drove his shadow-body backwards, Rhianna dragged Excalibur free and rolled sideways. Her strength returned and she sliced the horrid net from her ankles.

She stumbled to Elphin's side. Excalibur cut through the glowing ropes around his ankles and wrists just as easily, and she flung them away with a shudder. But her friend still lay as if dead on the altar, which gave her a problem. Could she carry him, as well as fight her way out of the chapel?

Mordred was still busy fending off the two ghosts, and she could hear the sounds of more fighting outside. As she hesitated, a body thudded against the locked door. "Hold on, Damsel Rhianna!" Sir Bors' voice called. "We're coming. We just got to deal with these bloodbeards first."

She had to get Elphin somewhere safer. Her gaze fell on the stairs winding up the tower. She sheathed Excalibur and heaved

Elphin over her shoulder. Being Avalonian, he was lighter than a human boy. She ran up the winding stair, trying not to think of his icy skin and the horrible web of Annwn that had stolen his strength. How long had he been bound with it?

"You'll be all right now, Elphin," she puffed. "Arianrhod's got the Grail of Stars on our ship. We'll get you back to the crystal caverns in Avalon, and they'll heal you in no time."

The bell at the top of the tower gave a clang, and she paused. The shadrake had been tethered to one of the pillars by more of the enchanted green ropes. As she appeared, it flung itself weakly towards her.

Rhianna carefully laid Elphin's limp body on the top step so that she could draw Excalibur again.

"Merlin?" she called warily. "Are you still in there?"

At first the shadrake did not reply, and her heart sank. Then it boomed, "JUST LIKE A DAMSEL! WHY DIDN'T YOU GET MY PATHFINDER OFF MORDRED WHILE YOU WERE DOWN THERE WITH HIM?"

Her heart missed a beat. She knelt by Elphin and felt around his neck, but the little spiral had gone. She thought of Mordred hiding his right hand under his cloak. She looked back down the winding stair and took a deep breath.

"I'll go back down and get it," she promised. "But we have to get Elphin to the ship first. He's not very heavy. Are you strong enough to carry him down there in your pouch? I'll join you as soon as I can."

She sliced through the ropes with Excalibur to free the dragon, and it flapped its great wings in relief.

"THE AVALONIAN PRINCE IS NOT IMPORTANT," it roared. "WE DO NOT NEED HIM NOW YOU HAVE FOUND THE FOUR LIGHTS. IN THIS BODY, I CAN CARRY THE PATHFINDER TO OPEN THE MISTS SO YOU MAY COMPLETE YOUR QUEST AND WAKE ARTHUR."

"Elphin is important to *me*!" Rhianna set her jaw. "If you won't carry him down to the ship, then I'm not going back to Avalon with you! King Arthur will just have to sleep for a thousand years, like Mordred always said he would. In the meantime, I'll make do with his ghost. It's almost as solid as a real person now,

335

and he cares for me, which is more than you seem to do. Maybe when you get fed up of flapping about in that dragon's body, you can do another of your druid spirit transfers into my father's body and bring King Arthur back yourself."

"FOOLISH CHILD. THAT IS NOT HOW THE SPIRIT MAGIC WORKS." The shadrake lashed its tail, making the bell clang again. "WE ARE WASTING TIME. YOU LURE MORDRED OUT OF THE CHAPEL, AND I WILL SOON GET THE PATHFINDER OFF HIM NOW I AM FREE OF MORGAN'S TRICKS. LEAVE THE AVALONIAN PRINCE HERE."

"No!" Rhianna said. At least the creature seemed more awake now that she'd freed it from the witch's ropes. "If you won't help me, then I'll get Elphin down there some other way."

She whistled for Alba, and her mare trotted around the hill followed by Evenstar. But the mist horses would not approach the tower while the shadrake was perched on it.

Bad thing eats horses, the mare said. *We go, be safe with herd!*

The two mist horses galloped back down the Tor, their tails flying.

"You're scaring them," Rhianna told Merlin with a frown. "Go away, if you're not going to help us."

"IT IS NOT ME. LOOK WHO HAS COME."

The green mist was thinning. Rhianna looked down and saw Uther's ghost-army fleeing across the water. She looked anxiously for the ship, and saw it drawn up on the beach where she and Cai had met the monks. Arianrhod stood at the rail with their packs at her feet, looking very small, while Gareth's ghost clung to the rigging and kept watch.

Smaller boats had been drawn up around the ship, and her heart lifted when she spotted Sir Bedivere and the squires who had ridden out to investigate Gareth's death, running up the path to help Sir Bors with the bloodbeards.

Then her heart gave an extra thud. Racing along the shore was a herd of white horses that glimmered in the mist, ridden by pale warriors led by a lord wearing a crown of leaves and berries in his dark hair.

"It's Lord Avallach!" she whispered. "With the Wild Hunt! The way between the worlds must be open again! Please, Merlin, help us just this once, and I promise I'll never put a hood on you or leash you to a perch, ever again."

The shadrake beat its wings and boomed, "I AM NOT A HAWK NOW."

Laughter came from below.

"I know you're up there, cousin!" Mordred called up the stair. "No escape that way, except for those who have wings! Met my dear father, have you? Blood always tells in the end. I did have my doubts for a moment back there, but the druid knows who is going to make the strongest Pendragon."

Rhianna looked uncertainly at the dragon. What if Merlin was working for the dark knight, after all? Before she could make up her mind, the shadrake's large claw reached past her and scooped up Elphin. She froze in sudden terror for her friend. But the creature slid the Avalonian prince gently into its pouch, as if he was a dragon-baby.

"I WILL CARRY HIM TO YOUR SHIP," it boomed. "PUT A HOOD ON ME AND LEASH ME TO A PERCH? HA HA, I WOULD LIKE TO SEE YOU TRY!"

The shadrake took off with a shriek of laughter. A shiver went down Rhianna's spine. Hoping Merlin would stay in control of the dragon long enough to fly Elphin to safety, she gripped Excalibur and headed back down the tower to get the pathfinder off her cousin.

◀ 10 ▶

Druid Blood

When druid flies on dragon's wing
And a damsel seeks to wake the king,
The spiral clutched in Mordred's fist
Will open their passage through the mist.

Rhianna took the stairs two at a time, Excalibur blazing in her hand. While she'd been in the belfry with the dragon, someone had beaten down the chapel door. The clash of blades echoed up the tower as men fought below. She paused on the final step and peered out cautiously to check the witch wasn't waiting to catch her in another enchanted net.

Sunlight, streaming through the broken door, showed men struggling between overturned benches – monks with their sticks and clubs against Mordred's blue-painted warriors from the north. The bloodbeards had better weapons, but the monks were angrier. Their leader picked up a bench and brought it down on the nearest bloodbeard's head, knocking the man senseless. Sir Bors leaped over the body, his sword flashing in a deadly arc as he yelled battle commands. Sir Bedivere followed with the squires, calling Rhianna's name.

She saw Cai in the thick of the fighting, trying to clear a path through the chapel with the Lance of Truth. He swung the weapon around wildly, scattering friends as well as enemies.

At first she couldn't see where Mordred had gone, and wondered if someone had finally managed to kill the dark knight. She felt a pang of disappointment – *she* wanted to be the one who avenged her father. Then she spotted her cousin crouched behind the altar, fiddling with something that glinted in the shadow of his cloak… the pathfinder he'd stolen from Elphin!

Anger filled her. She raised Excalibur and rushed towards him.

"Look out, Rhia – behind you!" Cai yelled.

Fearing another trap, she whirled around in time to see Morgan Le Fay's dark spirit rippling out of the shadows. A chill went down her back as the witch drew her enchanted green curtain closed around the altar, cutting them off from the noise of the fighting.

"Out of my way!" Rhianna ordered.

The witch hissed and shrank back from Rhianna's blade. "You must not take the Grail of Stars to Avalon!" she said. "You don't understand what you're doing."

"Yes I do!" Rhianna said. "I'm going to use it to bring my father back to life, and you're not going to stop me."

Excalibur's jewel blazed, and the spirits linked to her sword shimmered into view around her. The ghosts of Sir Galahad and Sir Percival came first, followed by the other men who had died in battle trying to save their king. The ghostly knights closed around Mordred's mother with angry expressions.

"You do not belong here, witch!" Galahad said. "Go back to Annwn."

Now Rhianna could see her father's ghost too, standing on the altar watching Mordred's hands. *"Quickly, daughter,"* he warned. *"He's opening the spiral path. He'll use it to escape again."*

Morgan Le Fay was backing away from the ghosts. Seeing her chance, Rhianna gripped Excalibur and leaped over the altar to land beside the dark knight.

Her cousin looked up. The pathfinder glittered in his right hand. The magic lit up his unnaturally handsome face and reflected in his green eyes.

He smiled at her. "Merlin's not the only one who can use this pathfinder, you know. Thanks to him, it turns out I have druid blood – at least, I have in this fist. Wish I'd known before, then maybe I'd have been able to stop your knights burning my old body. But my new one's so much better don't you think? More pleasing on the eye, as well as having the advantage of being invincible."

Rhianna shuddered. On the other side of altar, beyond the witch's green veil, she could see men falling and dying silently, as if she were watching one of Merlin's song-pictures back in Avalon. The surviving bloodbeards had retreated into the bell tower. Some of the monks rushed up after them, while the squires barricaded the chapel door with benches. She saw Sir Bors organising the rest of the monks – now better armed with their fallen enemies' swords and axes – to guard the windows.

She smiled grimly. "You're trapped, Mordred," she said. "Give me the pathfinder, and I'll ask my men to spare your life."

Her cousin glanced about the chapel and chuckled. "Men? You can't scare me with a bunch of squires and ghosts! I see only two living knights in your brave army, unless you count a half-grown boy who thinks a magic lance makes him into a champion."

He sneered at Cai, who was still trying to force his way towards them through Morgan Le Fay's enchantments with the Lance of Truth.

"Those monks out there follow just one master, and it's not your father, or any earthly king. They're not fighting for you, cousin, believe me! They want the Grail of Stars as much as anyone else. Do you think they're just going to let you sail off into the mists with it? The moment my bloodbeards are gone, they'll take it from you."

Rhianna frowned, thinking of Arianrhod waiting alone on the ship with the pack containing the fourth Light. "That's not true."

"Isn't it? They kept the Grail here once before, you know, when it first came to this land from across the sea. Before it disappeared into the mists. But we can still save it from them. Come with me along the spiral path, cousin, and let's use the four Lights together to rule the world." He extended his free hand.

Rhianna eyed the shadow-flesh, which blurred as she looked at it, changing from a boy's soft hand into a warrior's fist callused and scarred from carrying a weapon, and then into a six-fingered hand like Elphin's.

She shuddered and blinked away the illusion. "No."

Mordred sighed. "Very well then, I'll go

alone. We might have made a good team, you and I. But if you want your father to sleep in Avalon forever, and the shadrake to devour your fairy friend when it finally gets rid of Merlin's spirit, then that's up to you. Don't say I didn't give you the chance."

He closed his gauntlet around the pathfinder and muttered a spell under his breath. The air in the chapel shivered, and a deep note sounded as the bell rang above. Slowly at first, then faster and brighter, the magical path opened from the altar in a glowing green spiral through the overturned benches and groaning bodies, drawing up the witch's veil as it went.

Rhianna stared at that glowing route, reminded of when Merlin had opened the spiral path from the hawk mews in Camelot so she could confront her wounded cousin in his underground sanctuary. The monks guarding the windows crossed themselves as the creatures of Annwn that had been trying to snatch their souls were sucked, wailing, around the spiral and out of this world. Sir Galahad and Sir Percival were swept along on the ghostly tide, swinging their swords to continue their battle with those bloodbeards who had joined them in death.

Morgan Le Fay laughed as she followed them. "I'll await you in Annwn, my children," she called, blowing a kiss back to Rhianna and Mordred.

Rhianna's blood rose. Mordred grinned at her. The dark knight had begun to fade like a ghost, too. He was going to escape again, this time taking the pathfinder with him. Whether or not her cousin managed to get the Grail of Stars from Arianrhod, they needed the pathfinder to get Elphin through the mists and into Avalon's healing crystal caverns as soon as possible.

She sheathed Excalibur and stepped on to the glowing green path.

Sir Bors shouted, "Get away from him, Damsel Rhianna, *now*!"

Cai saw what she was about to do and yelled, "No, Rhia—!"

She grasped Mordred's left hand, and the chapel vanished.

❧❦❧

Rhianna's ears roared. This did not feel like her past journeys along the spiral path, which had been short and breathless but fairly painless. This time Mordred jerked her along in fits and starts, pulling her arm half out of its socket. His shadow-fingers clutched hers so tightly that she couldn't have let go of his hand, even if she'd wanted to.

Clearly her cousin could not use the pathfinder's magic as well as Merlin, despite his claim to druid blood.

The dark knight laughed. "No need to hold so tight, cousin. I won't let go of you."

As the last of the recently freed souls wailed past on the ghostly wind, Rhianna groped for Excalibur with her free hand, trying to reach the hilt and its magical jewel. But she couldn't get a grip on her sword. Panic rose. She thought her cousin had won, and they would both end up in Annwn.

Then a voice beside her ear said, "*Courage, daughter. I am with you. Use the Sword of Light to change the path.*" Her father's strong hand covered hers and guided it to the hilt. Warmth returned to her fingers. Her ears stopped roaring, and her stomach steadied.

She dragged Excalibur out of its scabbard. The blade shone through the mist, showing her the beach where they had landed with the villagers huddled nervously around their boats.

She took a deep breath, then another, and concentrated on the scene. Now she could smell the sea. The ship with its crooked mast loomed above her. She heard the shadrake flapping in a circle overhead, and then someone called her name.

"Rhia…? My lady…?"

"Arianrhod!" she whispered in relief. "Hold on, I'm coming."

With a final effort she sliced Excalibur

through the mist, and the bloodbeards' ghosts wailed onwards to Annwn without them, while Sir Galahad and Sir Percival rippled up to the deck.

Mordred hissed in anger, and his hand tightened about hers. "You're going nowhere without me, cousin."

With a sickening lurch, the spiral path deposited them both at the water's edge. Still gripping hands, they fell to their knees in the shallows. Rhianna gasped and spluttered as a wave hit her in the face. She struggled to pull her hand free so that she could reach the ship and her friend. The villagers rushed to help her. But Mordred sprang to his feet and jerked her up by her sore arm, pulling her against his shadow-body. He felt frighteningly strong.

"Stop!" he ordered. "Drop your sword!"

He twisted her arm behind her and jammed his other arm across her throat, dragging her towards the boats. The gauntlet containing the remains of his mortal fist stank. Rhianna's stomach heaved as pus oozed down her neck. The villagers looked desperately up the hill, where the monks who had gone with the knights and squires were racing out of the chapel, still too far away to help.

Awkwardly, Rhianna swung Excalibur's blade backwards, trying to reach the dark knight who held her captive. It was like swimming against a current. But she had trained at Camelot to use Excalibur with equal skill in either hand, whereas her cousin's other hand – the one across her throat – still gripped the pathfinder he'd used to bring them here.

"I *said* drop it!" Mordred hissed, giving her

captured arm another twist. "You can't win, cousin, not this time. I'm not a cripple any more, and I've got the pathfinder. I'm going to take the Grail and one of these boats, and you're going to tell the Wild Hunt to let me through the mists. Look, the dragon's here now – you can't fight us both."

From the corner of her eye she could see the shadrake, circling overhead with its bulging pouch. She hoped that meant Elphin was still safe inside it.

On the ship a pale-faced Arianrhod ducked, hugging her pack containing the Grail. "Don't let him have it, Lady Rhia!" she called.

"You can't win while *I* still hold one of the Lights," Rhianna said. Drawing on the strength of a hundred men from Excalibur's magical jewel, she gritted her teeth against the pain and wrenched her arm free.

She spun round to face her cousin. The arm he had twisted felt numb. She saw Mordred's lip curl as her sword hand shook. She waited until he tried to grab her again, then tossed the sword into her other hand and brought its blade down with all her strength across his right arm, just above the gauntlet. Excalibur must have remembered when King Arthur cut off the dark knight's hand in the battle of Camlann, because the sword sang in triumph as the mortal fist parted from its shadow-arm with a flash of green light, sending Mordred's homeless spirit howling up into the sky.

Rhianna's ears popped and she stumbled onto her knees, rubbing her sore arm. Her father's ghost reappeared and stared after the dark knight's spirit as it screamed away across the sea in a cloud of green stars. *"Oh well done, daughter!"* he said with pride. *"Your cousin won't recover from that in a hurry."*

⁂

Rhianna knelt on the beach, exhausted but grinning with pride. She'd beaten Mordred, despite his magic. Then black wings flapped overhead, reminding her she still didn't know how far they could trust Merlin.

She snatched up Mordred's dark fist before the shadrake could steal it away again. The gauntlet had clenched tightly about the pathfinder when the dark knight's body disintegrated. She used Excalibur to prise open the fingers, cringing as more pus oozed out. She clenched her teeth and picked the spiral out of the mess.

Cai was first to reach her, panting from his run down the hill. He swung the Lance of Truth in a wild circle. "Where did Mordred go?" he asked, scowling up and down the beach. "Let me kill him for you, Damsel Rhia!"

She ducked his lance with another grin. "Too late. He's gone."

Sir Bors puffed up behind the boy with Sir Bedivere and the squires, followed by the monks from the chapel, still looking for a fight. The villagers crowded round in relief and told them what had happened. When they realised Mordred had gone, the monks turned their attention to the ship. They pointed excitedly at the deck where Arianrhod's pack spilled white light across the water, showing up Gareth's ghosts. The maid lowered the ladder so the squires could scramble aboard.

They crowded around their dead friend all talking at once, full of their part in the battle.

Satisfied Rhianna was safe, Sir Bors sheathed his sword. "See what I mean?" he muttered to the monks. "That's the sort of crazy thing she does all time. I'm just glad she's nearly completed her quest, because it's enough to make an old knight's heart fail! C'mere..." He checked Rhianna up and down for damage, then opened his arms and swung her clean off her feet with his most enthusiastic hug yet.

Sir Bedivere smiled.

Rhianna looked anxiously over Sir Bors' shoulder to see what the monks were doing. Some of them had climbed aboard the ship after the squires. But they did not try to take the Grail as she'd feared. Instead, they lifted the broken mast and used the axes they had taken from the bloodbeards to begin fashioning a new, shorter one under Sir Galahad's ghostly instruction.

Finally Alba and Evenstar trotted up, whinnying anxiously.

We lose you in green light! said her mare. *We were frightened. Evenstar think dark dragon eat his rider! Is that an apple?*

The mare curled her lip in disgust at the sticky pathfinder. Rhianna laughed.

"No, my darling," she said, closing her fingers over the little spiral. "It's not an apple. But it'll take you to the best apples in Avalon! And that shadrake won't dare eat Elphin, or it'll have me to answer to."

She strode along the beach and glared up at the circling dragon. "Bring Elphin down to the beach, Merlin! We'll take him on the ship now.

I've got your pathfinder back, so you can open the way through the mists to Avalon for us."

Arianrhod blinked up at the shadrake as it descended. "I thought it was trying to steal Lady Nimue's cup for Mordred," she whispered. "I was so scared when he appeared like that right beside the ship! But I'm a Grail maiden now... and that means I must guard this cup with my life."

Rhianna smiled at her. "I know you will, Arianrhod. But there'll be no need for anyone to die protecting it. Mordred's finally gone, and the shadrake's helping us now..." She quickly explained to Sir Bedivere and the others how Merlin had helped fly the unconscious Elphin out of the chapel to safety.

The monks looked doubtful, but Cai grinned. "I *knew* Merlin wouldn't betray us!"

he said. "Is that really Elphin in the shadrake's pouch? It looks pregnant!"

"DRAGONS LAY EGGS, SILLY BOY," grumbled the shadrake, diving at Cai's head. The mist horses cantered off to a safe distance and watched with pricked ears as the boy ducked and swung the Lance of Truth to shoo the creature away.

The shadrake easily evaded the Lance and landed on the beach, spraying Cai with sand. It folded its wings with an exhausted grunt. "YOU MAY TAKE THE AVALONIAN BOY. HE IS GETTING HEAVY." It reached a claw into its pouch and hooked out Elphin's limp body.

Rhianna sheathed Excalibur and hurried to help her friend. Her heart pounded as she ducked beneath the shadrake's huge body, but it did not attack. Cai rushed up to help her pull Elphin clear, and together they carried their friend to the safety of the ship.

While the knights lifted the unconscious prince aboard, Rhianna gladly slipped the sticky pathfinder into the shadrake's pouch. She glimpsed the Crown of Dreams that Merlin had taken to bargain with Mordred glittering inside, and reached for that too.

"DO NOT BE GREEDY, RHIANNA PENDRAGON," the shadrake said, taking off again in another spray of sand. "YOU HAVE THE LIGHTS YOU NEED TO FINISH YOUR QUEST. I WILL KEEP ARTHUR'S CROWN SAFE UNTIL HE RETURNS TO CAMELOT."

"That won't be long now!" Rhianna called, pulling a face at the dragon.

She packed her cousin's rotting fist carefully into her saddlebag and vaulted on to Alba. She wished they had time to burn the horrid thing before they left the Tor, but that would hold them up. Meanwhile, Cai climbed aboard the ship with the Lance of Truth and helped the other squires up the rope ladder. Evenstar put his nose over the rail, trying to reach his enchanted rider.

"Tell him Elphin's going to be all right now," Rhianna told her mare. "We're taking him to the crystal caverns so his father can heal him." She hated to think what Lord Avallach would say when he saw what Mordred had done to his son. But Alba must have passed the message on, because Evenstar pricked his ears and whinnied.

She checked everyone was safely on board,

and patted Alba. "We're ready to go, Merlin!" she called. "Don't fly too fast."

The shadrake flapped away over the water, and the mist began to sparkle. The ship drew away from the beach to follow. The monks muttered uneasily when they saw the magical spiral path open beneath the dragon. But Gareth's mother stumbled up to Rhianna, her eyes shining. "Thank you for bringing my boy back, Princess," she said. "I know he's no longer part of this world, but he's promised to stay with me until my time comes to leave it so we can go to the next one together."

She hugged her son's ghost. Gareth rippled through his mother's arms to escape the embrace and winked at Rhianna.

Rhianna bit her lip. "Thank you for helping Elphin," she mumbled in return, thinking guiltily of how she'd tried to stop the knights riding to the Lonely Tor's aid.

"I hope the fairy lad gets better soon," Gareth's mother said.

"So do I," Rhianna whispered, and galloped Alba after the ship to catch up with her friends.

❁

She found Evenstar trotting next to the rail so he could keep an anxious eye on his rider. Elphin lay on the deck, wrapped in Sir Bors' cloak. Arianrhod knelt beside the prince, strumming the broken harp and singing softly to him.

Rhianna experienced a pang of jealousy. She should be the one watching over Elphin. What if he woke, and the first face he saw was Arianrhod's? But she couldn't guard the ship and nurse her friend at the same time.

The maid glanced up at her and smiled. "He's looking much better already, my lady! It's like he knows he's going home. Is King Arthur's ghost still here?"

Rhianna frowned. In all the excitement, she'd forgotten they needed to take King Arthur's soul back to Avalon so it could return to its body, as well as the Grail to work the magic that would restore it. When was the last time she'd seen her father's ghost? He'd been with her when she and Mordred fought on the beach. He'd helped her draw her sword, and he'd praised her when she had cut off Mordred's dark fist and sent her cousin's shadow-body spinning after the other souls to Annwn.

"Father?" she whispered. "Are you there?"

She peered uneasily into the sparkling mist

behind them. Did she have time to gallop back around the spiral and look for him before the path closed?

I am very fast, Alba reminded her. *I will go back if you want.*

"I know you are, my darling, but he might already be in Avalon waiting for us, and Uther's ghosts might still be out there—"

As she spoke, a boat appeared out of the mist. A figure wearing a hooded cloak clutched the sides, while a knight in salt-stained armour crouched in the bows peering at the water.

Wearily, she drew her sword. "We're being followed!" she warned.

The figure in the boat looked up. Eyes gleamed in the shadow of its hood as a pale finger pointed at Rhianna.

Oars rose and fell, splashing crazily as the

boat lurched towards them. Its crew were clumsy rowers, but the Grail ship with its ragged sails and shortened mast could not outrun them. Though she barely had the energy to raise her blade, Rhianna trotted Alba between the two vessels. She wasn't going to let anyone take the fourth Light from her, not now.

Then the knight opened his helm, and his silver hair blew free in the spray.

"Put your sword away, Princess!" he called. "I'm not letting you sail off into the mists on that ship of ghosts a second time, no matter how much magic you use on me. I swore an oath to protect whoever holds Excalibur, which means you, Princess, even if you saw fit to give my lance to young Cai last year." He squinted at the deck, where Cai stood in the stern beside Sir Bors, gripping the Lance of Truth. "Is the lad still alive? Miracles will never cease."

"Sir Lancelot!" Rhianna said, lowering her sword in relief. She gave the hooded figure a closer look and her heart missed a beat. "Mother...?" she whispered.

"About bloody time you turned up, Lancelot!" Sir Bors called, not recognising the queen in her disguise. "What were you doing, while we were seeing off Mordred and his bloodbeards with nothin' but a bunch of monks armed with sticks? Enjoying a picnic with the damsels back at Camelot?"

"Looking for Rhianna, of course," Sir Lancelot grumbled. "It's not my fault if she vanished off the face of the earth. Your mother was frantic with worry when you sailed away into the mist on the Grail ship, Princess. She thought you'd die like Galahad and the rest. She insisted on coming with us, but by the time we rode out again we couldn't find a trace of any of you. It wasn't until I had a dream of Rhianna fighting Mordred in the church on the Lonely Tor we had an idea where to look. Agravaine's here, too. We came as fast as we could. Throw us a rope, Bors! We're not rowing all the way across to Avalon."

The knights on the ship gaped at Queen Guinevere as she pushed back her hood and raised her chin to meet their stares.

Cai grinned and lowered the ladder. "That dream was Damsel Rhia calling us all with Excalibur's magic! But then she went and killed the dark knight all on her own, so it's safe enough, Your Majesty. All we got to do now is wake King Arthur. Mordred's finished."

But as Sir Lancelot's men climbed aboard,

a twist of darkness rushed past the ship, making Excalibur's jewel blaze brightly and sending a shiver down Rhianna's spine. She thought of the dark fist in her saddlebag and the task still ahead of her, and looked uneasily at the queen.

DARK DRAGON

Terror gripped Mordred. His cousin had taken his mortal fist, and with it his last chance of remaining in the world of men.

"Mother!" he wailed, as his shadow body disintegrated and his spirit was sucked with the other ghosts towards the dark realm of Annwn. "Help me!"

But he had no way of reaching her. Rhianna had seen to that when she'd used Excalibur to separate his mortal fist from his shadow-body. It felt a bit like when the knights had burned his crippled body at Camelot. But this time there was no handy dragon for him to spirit-ride to freedom, because the shadrake's body was already occupied… by the druid.

Merlin had tricked him!

Fury overcame his terror, and he concentrated the last of his strength on the dragon. Darkness… a sickening lurch… then he too was inside the shadrake's body, looking out through its eyes as it flapped over the water.

He saw the spiral path far below, sparkling in the mist. His cousin rode her fairy horse along it with Excalibur shining in her hand. On the ship, the Grail of Stars shone so brightly that Mordred could not see who was on board, though he had a fair idea.

The fairy prince, that idiot squire who carried the Lance of Truth, his mother's ex-maid, and Arthur's knights… he should have killed the lot of them while he had the chance. His cousin would never have got this far without her friends.

Then Merlin noticed him, and the shadrake's body shuddered as their spirits clashed.

"It's too late, Mordred!" the druid growled. "There's nowhere for you to go now, except the eternal darkness of Annwn. Get out of this body before I throw you out."

"I'm not going to let you take the four Lights to Avalon and bring Arthur back," Mordred said. "The throne of Camelot is *mine!*"

"Not for long. The way to Avalon is open."

"It can easily be closed again," Mordred hissed.

He used all the tricks his mother had

taught him, trying to turn the dragon. But Merlin fought him every wing beat of the way. The shadrake shrieked in protest as its body tried to fly in two directions at once. It twisted in the air and somersaulted, sending a few smaller pieces of treasure falling from its pouch into the sea.

Mordred forced the dragon's claw towards its pouch, searching for the spiral pathfinder.

But Merlin's spirit was too strong, and the claw slowly withdrew. The dragon swooped back up into the sky and turned another somersault. This time, its pouch stayed open and more treasure fell out in a sparkling rain. Mordred laughed in triumph when he saw the silver spiral follow the rest, glinting as it vanished into the mist far below.

"You've lost, Merlin!" he said. "Even if

they reach Avalon, my cousin Rhianna and her friends will never find their way back to the world of men without your druid charm."

Merlin made a frustrated sound. "You forget the Wild Hunt can ride through these mists."

"They can't ride anywhere if the mists between worlds are closed to them by a greater power. If the Grail of Stars is on that ship, all I need to do is sink it. King Arthur will never return to Camelot, and his daughter will be trapped in Avalon for all time."

Mordred felt the druid's spirit waver, and made another attempt to take control of the dragon. This time it worked. He got the huge wings folded and then retreated into a dark corner of the shadrake's mind.

Wind whistled past the creature's scales as

it dived towards the ship far below. He sensed Merlin trying to make the shadrake unfold its wings and pull up. As he'd guessed, the druid was trying to save those on the ship, as well as the dragon's body.

Mordred, on the other hand, did not care if they all died.

He kept his mind clamped tight shut and refused to think of what would happen to his spirit when the dragon drowned. If he ended up in Annwn, he'd take those on the ship and three of the Lights with him. A pity Rhianna wasn't on board with the others. But Excalibur alone would do his cousin little good, even if she did make it through the mists alive.

"You might reach Avalon, cousin," he whispered. "But you'll never see your friends again."

Sea Battle

Their ship sailed swiftly into the west
On the final stage of Rhianna's quest,
One last battle must our damsel fight
To keep the fourth and greatest Light.

As they neared Avalon, Alba scented the Wild Hunt's horses in the mist and neighed, fighting for her head. Rhianna wanted nothing more than to overtake the ship and gallop on ahead. But she held the mare on a tight rein, remembering how Morgan Le

Fay had ambushed them the last time they had come this way.

"No, my darling," she whispered. "We have to stay and protect my mother and the others."

She rode with her sword in her hand as half-seen shadows flickered around them. They had lost sight of their dragon guide some time ago, and Excalibur's blade still gleamed faintly in warning. But she was no longer an untrained damsel. If Mordred's witch-mother tried any tricks today, she'd be ready.

Something shiny splashed into the sea nearby, making the little mare snort and shake her mane. A few more glittering pieces splashed around them, like someone throwing stones. *It rains silver,* Alba said, sidestepping nervously.

Rhianna looked up with a frown. "Merlin?"

she called. "Are you still up there? Is everything all right?"

More glittering missiles hissed down, and some rattled on the deck of the ship. The knights looked up in alarm. Then the shadrake reappeared directly overhead with an angry screech. Green and purple sparks trailed from its wings as it somersaulted through the clouds. Lancelot's men reached for their swords. Sir Lancelot pulled Guinevere's hood back up to cover her bright hair and hurried the queen below.

"It's all right!" Rhianna called, frowning at the dragon's antics. "The shadrake's on our side. It's opening the spiral path for us—"

Bad thing will eat us! Her mare said, misting suddenly from under her. Rhianna was holding Excalibur so she did not fall off, but she couldn't make the agitated Alba approach the ship. Evenstar seemed upset now too, misting in and out of view as he cantered around the ship in circles.

"What's wrong, silly?" she said. "Merlin's in control of the dragon now. I don't know what he's up to, but he won't let it eat you."

As she spoke, the shadrake plummeted out of the clouds, its wings folded and its red eye fixed firmly on the ship. Her unease returned as Excalibur blazed again. She'd just killed Merlin's son… maybe Mordred was right, and blood did tell in the end? The druid might have lured them out here to kill them all.

"No!" she shouted.

Putting her heels into Alba's sides, she urged the mare back across the water, determined not to let the shadrake sink the ship.

They were too far away. The dragon was falling like a black rock towards the deck, making no attempt to unfurl its wings.

Alba stubbornly dug her hooves into the water. *Want to follow Evenstar!* she neighed, trying to turn round again.

Rhianna gritted her teeth and raised the flat of her blade over the mare's hindquarters. She had never hit Alba, and didn't want to hurt the little horse. But she wouldn't watch the shadrake drown her mother and her friends so close to the shore of Avalon and the end of her quest! Then she remembered she was a Pendragon. That meant she could talk to dragons even if Merlin's spirit was no longer helping them. Maybe the creature's own spirit was still in there somewhere.

She lowered Excalibur and took a deep

breath. "Shadrake!" she called in dragon-speech. "Can you hear me? You're going to die if you don't use your wings. Pull up!"

The dragon continued its suicidal dive.

On the ship, Arianrhod crouched protectively over the unconscious Elphin. Cai stood bravely beside them, the Lance of Truth aimed at the diving dragon. Sir Bors and Sir Lancelot were organising the men to brace their swords on the deck, blades pointing at the sky. The shadrake would meet a bloody end if it did not pull out of its dive, but the ship would still sink, with everyone she loved on board. She saw Sir Galahad and Sir Percival rippling around the tattered sails, trying to turn the vessel to avoid the crash.

"Shadrake!" she called again, wishing she still had the Crown of Dreams. "Lord Avallach and his Wild Hunt will take your dragon-soul if you die out here. Fly back to Annwn where you'll be safe!"

She had no idea if dragons had souls, but her words seemed to reach the creature. Its tail lashed, and one wing unfurled.

"That's right!" she shouted in encouragement. "You can do it! You're stronger than Merlin, if he's making you do this."

It made her furious to think her father's druid had lured them onto the spiral path between worlds, just so that he could betray them at the last moment.

The shadrake twisted in midair and roared in amusement, "MERLIN IS NOT CONTROLLING THE BEAST NOW! DO YOU NOT RECOGNISE ME, COUSIN? YOU FORCED MY SPIRIT

INTO THIS BODY WHEN YOU DESTROYED MY SHADOW ONE. IT IS A BIT CROWDED IN HERE BUT I AM STRONGER THAN THE DRUID."

"*Mordred*!" Rhianna whispered. Now she understood why the dragon had been acting so strangely. She wondered what had happened to Merlin's spirit, and a chill went through her as she realised her cousin was back in control of the spiral path. But the dark knight had a weakness. She waved her sword to distract the creature and galloped Alba away from the ship, yelling, "Want the Sword of Light, do you cousin? Come and get it!"

The shadrake missed the shortened mast by a talon's length and changed course to dive at Rhianna. It was working. She crouched over her horse's neck. "Faster, Alba!"

she said, heading the mare into the mist.

Then Cai shouted behind her, "Look out!"

She glanced back over her shoulder, afraid the shadrake had decided to sink the ship first and come after Excalibur later. But the warning hadn't been meant for her. She watched in horror as the water around the ship erupted with glittering fish-tails and green hair.

Fish-people! her mare said. *They are angry with us for taking their shining cup.*

Distracted by the shadrake's attack, no one had seen them coming. The fish-people pushed against the hull with their webbed hands, forcing the ship off its sparkling path, which was fading now that the shadrake had come after Rhianna. She saw the knights grab their swords and lean over the rail to fend off this new threat, while Cai jabbed at the green heads with the Lance of Truth. Then a webbed hand caught the end of the Lance, and the boy vanished over the stern with a little scream.

"Cai!" Rhianna gasped, by now too far away to help her friends.

But Sir Lancelot had caught hold of the boy's arm as he fell. Between the champion knight's slashing blade and Cai's kicking feet, the two of them made it back to the safety of the deck. Cai no longer had the Lance, and Rhianna's heart sank when she saw it floating in the water among all the flashing fish-tails.

"Give that back!" she yelled, urging her mare towards the ship. She gripped Excalibur tightly in case the fish-people tried to take the Sword of Light, too.

She'd forgotten the shadrake. As she turned Alba, its jaws opened and ice crackled out in a blue cloud, freezing the water around her mist horse's hooves.

Rhianna raised her shield over her head, desperately hoping it would protect her mare.

Alba tried to mist out of the way but failed. *Help!* she whinnied. *I am stuck.*

"I know you are, my darling," Rhianna said, pointing Excalibur at the dragon. "Don't worry, I won't let the beast hurt you."

At least the ice meant the fish-people in the water couldn't reach her mare's legs. She put them out of her mind and braced herself as the shadrake swooped closer.

Taking a deep breath, she lowered her shield and shouted up at the creature in dragon-speech, "I know you carry the Crown of Dreams in your pouch! I don't need it any more. You can keep the third Light and earn freedom for dragons everywhere, if you'll just carry Prince Mordred's spirit into Annwn for me... And release Merlin, if he's still spirit-riding you," she added quickly.

The shadrake pulled out of its dive and shook its huge head as if it had a fly stuck in its ear.

"YOU CAN'T GIVE... IT... THE CROWN..., COUSIN!" Mordred's voice spluttered.

"I'm not talking to *you*!" Rhianna shouted back. "I'm talking to the shadrake!"

More ice crackled from the shadrake's mouth. But her Avalonian armour protected her from its deadly breath, and the plume of ice passed around her to freeze several more of the fish-people attacking the ship.

While the other fish-people swam to help

their trapped friends, Cai leaped off the ship and ran along the frozen path to retrieve the Lance of Truth. He slipped on the ice, regained his balance, and jabbed the glittering point at the shadrake.

"Yah!" he yelled. "Get away from Princess Rhianna, you beast!"

The shadrake snapped at the Lance, but missed. It turned another somersault as the rival spirits fought for control of its body, and smashed a hole in the ice with a huge claw, releasing Alba. The little mare cantered out of the way, shaking her head in relief.

Rhianna looked anxiously for Cai. But he had already run back across the cracking ice to the ship, where the knights helped him and the Lance back on board – only just in time. The final slab of ice slid under the keel and was crushed to pieces.

Cai grinned at her, swinging his lance at the escaping fish-people. "Don't stand still, Damsel Rhianna!" he called. "Or you'll get stuck again."

Rhianna trotted Alba in circles. "Well?" she called to the shadrake, before Mordred could win back control of the beast. "Do we have a bargain?"

She held her breath.

"IT IS A GOOD BARGAIN, PENDRAGON MAID," boomed the shadrake. "I SHALL TAKE THIS CROWN BACK TO MY LAIR SO DRAGONS EVERYWHERE CAN BE FREE. NO PUNY HUMAN SPIRIT CONTROLS *ME!*"

She let out her breath in relief as the creature splashed across the water, half swimming and half flying. Finally it gained height and flapped away into the mist, icicles glittering from its tail. She just hoped it would remember to release Merlin's spirit before it reached Annwn.

But the danger wasn't over yet. Now that the dragon had gone, more slabs of ice were lifting from the water, pushed from underneath by the angry fish-people. Alba snorted at the ice, picking her hooves up high. Evenstar bucked and kicked as the webbed hands tried to catch his legs and tail.

I fight too! Alba snorted, kicking at the green heads as they surfaced around her.

Rhianna recognised some of the fish-girls who had been sitting with Lady Nimue at the feast. She hauled on the reins. "No, Alba! Don't fight – let me talk to them."

She checked the deck to make sure Arianrhod and the Grail were safe. The maid still crouched beside Elphin, clutching her pack and staring at the water in fear. The cup was glittering again. Rainbows spilled out between Arianrhod's fingers, flashing from the knights' armour and bathing Elphin's sleeping face. The prince lay wrapped in Sir Bors' cloak, as helpless as when they'd taken him on board. Rhianna tried not to think what would happen to her friends if Nimue's people managed to sink the ship.

Some of the fish-people were now climbing the rails, hauling themselves up by their strong swimmers' arms. The knights tried to push them back, but there were too many of them. As fast as one body flopped back into the water, ten more climbed up to replace it. Cai swung the Lance at their grasping hands, but although it sparkled fiercely its magic seemed to have no effect on Nimue's people. The fish-people's tails flapped on deck as they tried to take the second Light from the boy. Arianrhod stared at Rhianna, wide-eyed, holding the cup they had stolen from the Grail Castle high as the webbed hands reached towards it.

"What shall I do, my lady?" she called.

Rhianna looked desperately at the magical path Merlin had opened for them through the mists. It was fading fast now the shadrake and the pathfinder had gone. But a familiar jetty sparkled in the haze ahead... the same jetty where she and Elphin had raced their mist horses while they were growing up, the furthest they had been able to ride without crossing the sea into the land of men.

Her heart gave a lurch of joy. "Avalon!" she breathed.

Alba forgot to be scared of the fish-people and snatched at the reins in excitement. *Home!* she whinnied.

"Throw the Grail to me!" Rhianna instructed.

She sheathed Excalibur so that she could catch the cup. Arianrhod eyed the distance doubtfully. Then a fish-girl grabbed the maid's ankle, and Arianrhod flung the shining Light over the water towards Rhianna and Alba.

Not hard enough.

As its light faded, the cup dropped towards the waves, where the fish-people swam to catch it. The ones on the ship dived over the rail after it, too.

"That's *mine!*" Rhianna yelled, digging her heels into Alba's ribs.

The little mare leaped forwards. *You do*

not have to kick me like that, she snorted. *I am very fast.*

The fish-tails came together in a thrashing whirlpool beneath the falling cup. But Alba was faster. With a fierce squeal, the mare flattened her ears and charged into the scrum with bared teeth. Rhianna leaned down and caught the cup just before it splashed into the water. She snatched it clear of the grasping hands and pulled herself back into the saddle.

"Don't mist, Alba," she said through gritted teeth as her mare carried her through the churning tails into clear water. "I'm not holding Excalibur any more."

It is all right, the mare said. *You hold the shining cup.*

Rhianna cast a quick look back to check her friends were safe. Seeing the ship start to move forwards again as the wind filled its sails, she smiled grimly. The Grail had been what the fish-people wanted. They were all chasing her now, leaving the Lance with Cai so he could help the others protect the queen. The further she led them from the ship, the safer her friends and her mother would be. She crouched low over Alba's neck and urged the mare towards the jetty.

"Race the fish-people, Alba!" she shouted.

><8><

It was a wild race.

Rhianna could barely see through the water in her eyes, her mare's flying mane, and the light blazing from the cup she clutched against her armour. She grinned as the jetty loomed closer. The fish-people swam fast, but Alba galloped faster.

I smell apples! Alba said, pricking her ears at the beach where the Wild Hunt's horses crowded the shore. Rhianna gripped the Grail tighter, preparing herself to face Lord Avallach. But Alba shied as a green head surfaced right under her nose, the hair glistening with coloured lights. Rhianna almost lost her balance. She fumbled for Excalibur, holding the Grail awkwardly.

She couldn't think how the fish-people had got ahead of her. Then she recognised Queen Nimue, whose turquoise eyes held her gaze until Rhianna slid her sword back into its scabbard. She could not hurt Nimue, who had helped her so often in the land of men, even if the fish-lady *had* tricked her into wearing the Crown of Dreams in the Grail Castle. Rhianna felt a bit guilty that she hadn't waited for an explanation before stealing the cup and fleeing on the ship.

Lady Nimue shook her head sadly. "I knew you were a wild one, Rhianna Pendragon. But I never had you down as a thief. Did you think you could just steal one of my magic cups and I would not notice?"

Rhianna glanced at the dented goblet she held. "I didn't think you'd miss it," she mumbled. "Arianrhod told me you had lots of prettier ones."

She could see some of the Avalonians she'd grown up with, running through the woods to see who had opened the mists. She wondered if she could throw the cup as far as the jetty.

The fish-people caught up and formed a circle around Alba, moving their tails lazily to keep their heads above water. Rhianna tried to ride the mare closer to the shore, but the fish-people massed together, forming a scaly barrier between her and the beach.

The little mare snorted and backed off.

"Come now," Lady Nimue said, shaking her head at Rhianna again. "You can do better than that. You know that's no ordinary cup you drank from. A princess of Camelot has no need to steal a dented goblet."

"All right!" Rhianna admitted. "I thought it was the Grail of Stars, and I thought you'd tried to poison me, so I took it before it could turn me into a ghost like Sir Galahad and the others. I need it to wake my father. I promise I'll give it back afterwards, but I'm not going to let you stop me now. So please let me pass. I don't want to hurt you."

Nimue laughed. "That's better! More what

I'd expect from a girl with Pendragon blood. I didn't give you poison to drink, silly, or you'd be dead by now. It was merely a potion to help you find the answer to my riddle – your Grail test, which you did not complete. So how do you know if you have the right Grail?"

Rhianna's heart missed a beat. She looked at the cup more carefully. It had stopped shining, and looked ordinary again. "The *right* Grail?" she said, frowning. "What do you mean?"

"There are many Grails," the fish-lady said gently. "One for each person who undertakes a Grail Quest, as all seek something different. Sir Galahad made his choice. So did young Percival. They chose to remain in the Fisher King's castle so they could stay together for all time. Your quest is different. That's why I asked you a special riddle of your own...

What does the Grail contain?"

"I've already answered that one!" Rhianna said, scowling at the fish-people who surrounded her. "I told your Guardians when they tried to stop us leaving – didn't they tell you?"

She should tell Alba to mist through the fish-people while she could still see the shore of Avalon. Lord Avallach would surely help her. But what if she had chosen the wrong Grail?

She looked back the way she had come, undecided. She could no longer see the ship in the mist, and her stomach fluttered. She hoped her friends and the knights hadn't got lost in the mist between worlds.

"Tell me yourself," Nimue said.

"Nothing, see!" Rhianna turned the cup upside down to demonstrate. "It's a trick question."

Lady Nimue gave her a sad look. "Why do you think that?"

Rhianna set her jaw. "Whatever you gave me to drink spilled out when Arianrhod threw it across your hall, and I haven't put anything else into it yet. So let me through! I'll soon find out if it's the right Grail or not, when I take it to the crystal caverns and use it to give my father water from the Moon Pool to drink, like Merlin said."

Lady Nimue laughed her tinkling laugh. "Don't give up easily, do you? Nor old Merlin! I gather he tried to spirit-ride that shadrake — more fool him. So the druid told you how to use it, did he? Well then, the answer should be obvious. Don't look so worried, Rhianna Pendragon. It's not a trick question, and now you've defeated Mordred there's no reason you shouldn't borrow it. I just need to know you'll use its power in the right way. Answer correctly, and I'll let you pass. What does the Grail contain?"

Rhianna stared in frustration at the cup she held. She still couldn't see anything inside it. She cast another desperate glance at Avalon's shore. She had not come this far to fail now.

She started to gather up her reins. Then she grew still as two ghostly arms slid around her waist.

I carry King Arthur as well! Alba said. *He is very light.*

Rhianna's breath caught in her throat as her father's ghost whispered in her ear, "*What do you want it to contain, daughter?*"

She thought of how his arms would feel, warm and alive, and imagined his breath on the back of her neck. She thought of her mother, who had insisted on coming with Sir Lancelot to find her. She thought of Elphin lying on the ship, enchanted by the dark magic of Annwn. And suddenly she knew the answer. Sir Galahad's and Sir Percival's Grails had brought them death, but they had chosen to become ghosts so they could stay together. Hers might be a different choice, as Lady Nimue said, but the answer was the same.

The fish-queen smiled at her. "Well, Rhianna Pendragon? Your father is waiting. The shadrake flies to Annwn with the Crown of Dreams. The Wild Hunt guards the shores of Avalon. We haven't time to sit out here in the mist between worlds, playing riddle games."

"Love," she said, as her father's arms tightened into a ghostly hug. "The answer's love!"

◀12▶

Avalon

Fair Avalon's shore sparkled ahead
When Rhianna came to wake the dead.
Brave damsel seeks to end her quest
But will she pass the final test?

ady Nimue smiled. "Congratulations,
Rhianna Pendragon. The cup you took
from my castle has magic enough for your
purpose. You may take it to Avalon and use it
as you wish, but be warned – after it has been
filled, its magic will work only once. I'll meet

you at the Moon Pool so you can return it when you have completed your quest."

With a splash of her tail, the fish-queen slipped beneath the surface and vanished underwater, followed by the rest of her people.

Rhianna looked warily at the Wild Hunt waiting for her on the beach.

"*Well done, daughter*," said her father, giving her waist another ghostly squeeze. "*You do not need to fear Avallach's people. Hold your head high. Remember you carry what they dare not touch. I'll meet you tonight. I had better not tempt the fairy lord's Hunt with my soul.*" His arms faded, and he left her on a breath of warm wind.

Alba pricked her ears at the jetty and shook her mane. Rhianna held the little mare back. Part of her was as impatient as Alba. She wanted to gallop as fast as she could to Lord

Avallach's palace and take the Grail straight down to the crystal caverns to wake her father. But Merlin had said she must wait until the stars were out before she filled the cup at the Moon Pool, and the sun still shone on Avalon's golden wood. After all that she and her friends had been through to find the Grail, she didn't want to ruin the magic by getting the timing wrong. And now that she was back, she felt nervous about meeting the Avalonians again, who had teased her for her lack of magic when they had been growing up.

Alba fidgeted and pawed at the water. *What is wrong?*

"Nothing, my darling." Rhianna patted the mare's sweaty neck. "We're waiting for the others, that's all. They might get lost."

Alba snorted. *They are not lost. Evenstar*

is coming. I want my apples! You promised.

By this time, the ship had emerged from the end of the spiral path. With a loud neigh, Evenstar galloped past them to the beach, where he bucked wildly, as if trying to dislodge a rider, before stopping to talk to the mist horses ridden by the green-clad Avalonian hunters. Lord Avallach rode the leading horse, a bow slung across his back. He stared at the ship with purple eyes, and Rhianna shivered. She knew exactly who the Avalonian lord was looking for.

Drawing herself up straight in Alba's saddle, she raised the Grail before her. The cup flashed in the Avalonian sun, filling her eyes with rainbows that reflected in the water all around them.

She took a deep breath. "All right, Alba. Time to go home."

✿

The Avalonians drew back to let her through as she trotted Alba up the beach to meet the Hunt. They stared curiously at the cup she held. Those on the jetty finished securing the ship. The knights and Queen Guinevere disembarked and gazed about them in wonder.

Cai jumped eagerly off the jetty to join Rhianna, tripped over the Lance of Truth and fell flat on his face in the sand. He picked himself up, red-faced. But nobody noticed the boy's embarrassment. They were all watching the Hunt, which had formed a snorting, stamping circle to watch Rhianna and Lord Avallach meet.

Alba whinnied to Lord Avallach's stallion, which blew gently into the mare's nostrils to welcome her home. Rhianna licked her dry lips and met the Avalonian lord's purple gaze. After her stay in the land of men, his wild black hair and crown of berries seemed very alien.

"*Faha'ruh*, Lord Avallach," she said, showing him the dented cup. "I've found the Grail of Stars! And I've got Excalibur back, and my champion Cai here carries the Lance of Truth." She beckoned to Cai, who squeezed nervously through the mist horses to join them, gripping his lance. "But I'm afraid we... er... lost the Crown of Dreams to a dragon on our way here," Rhianna continued. "We lost Merlin, too."

She wondered what had happened to the druid. Was his spirit still trapped in the shadrake's body with Mordred's?

Lord Avallach barely glanced at the cup she held. "Where is my son?" he asked.

Rhianna looked at the ship, where Elphin still lay motionless on the deck. Arianrhod knelt at his side, trying to explain to the Avalonians on the jetty what was wrong with their prince.

"He's still alive, Lord Avallach," Rhianna said quickly. "But he was captured by Mordred and bound with enchanted ropes from Annwn. We've brought him home so you can lift the spell..." Her voice faltered. "You *can* lift the spell, can't you?"

The Avalonian lord's eyes darkened. "Annwn's magic causes us more pain than any mortal weapon," he said. "I warned Elphin he would get hurt if he stayed in the land of men, but he wouldn't listen to me. You stole him away with your human charms, so now he's paying the price. I was afraid something like this would happen."

Rhianna flinched. "I'm sorry," she whispered. "It was my fault. I didn't realise the danger he was in, or I'd have rescued him before I went to look for the Grail."

Lord Avallach's gaze rested on the glittering cup she held. "Not so easily, I suspect. At least you seem to have found what you were looking for. And I see Queen Guinevere has graced us with her presence, too." He sighed. "What's done cannot be undone. Let's get Elphin into the crystal caverns, and see if that grail you've found can wake King Arthur. Then maybe you'll take your knights and your family back to the land of men, and leave us all in peace."

Rhianna relaxed slightly as Lord Avallach raised a hand and his hunters drew their horses aside to let her and Cai pass. A horse was brought for Guinevere, and the Avalonian lord rode across to the jetty to greet the queen. The knights helped Arianrhod lift Elphin off the ship and laid the unconscious prince gently over Evenstar's back. The little horse bent his head to sniff his limp rider and whinnied sadly.

He thinks his rider might sleep for ever, Alba told her.

Rhianna's heart jumped. "No," she said, watching one of the Avalonian boys take Evenstar's rein to lead him along the woodland trail behind Lord Avallach and the queen. "Elphin will be all right now he's home. The crystal caverns will heal him, just like they used to heal me when we were little. He'll be better in no time, you'll see."

"And he's going to be dead impressed when he hears we've sent Mordred's spirit to Annwn, found the Grail of Stars and woken

King Arthur!" Cai said, running alongside Alba. "That'll show him humans don't need fairy magic to finish quests!" He tripped over his lance again and winced. "Do you have to ride so fast, Damsel Rhianna? We don't know these woods like you do, remember."

Seeing her friends and the knights were getting left behind, Rhianna slowed the mare so they could catch up. Arianrhod carried Elphin's harp, the broken string twanging softly as it bounced on her back. "I'm going to see if I can find someone to mend this harp so Elphin can show us those song pictures you told us about," the maid explained with a smile. "I'd like to see some magic before we go back to Camelot."

Rhianna grimaced at the thought of another ballad about her, complete with life-sized pictures in the walls of Lord Avallach's palace for her mother and everyone else to see. "Maybe we shouldn't heal Elphin too quickly," she said. "I'd like some time alone with my father before the whole of Avalon starts watching us."

"You'll be lucky!" Cai said. "Everyone's going to want to watch you bring King Arthur back from the dead. It'll be even more exciting than his wedding to Queen Guinevere."

"You're too young to remember King Arthur's wedding," Arianrhod said.

"Well, everyone knows how much food there was," Cai said. "The squires say Camelot was just as beautiful and safe as Avalon in those days, before Mordred joined the Round Table and started plotting with his witch-mother to take the throne. And it'll be safe and beautiful again when we return with King Arthur. We'll be heroes!"

"And heroines," Rhianna said, exchanging a smile with Arianrhod.

Maybe it would be all right, she thought. They had reached Avalon with three of the Lights. All she had to do now was fill her grail from the Moon Pool and take it into the crystal caverns to wake her father. *The cup has magic enough for your purpose*, Lady Nimue had said. Did that mean she would succeed in her quest to bring her father back to Camelot?

"Watch yourself, Damsel Rhianna," Sir Bors muttered, interrupting her thoughts. "I don't like the way them Avalonians are lookin' at you."

She followed his gaze and saw her childhood rivals casting glances at her and whispering together in the trees.

In spite of a mounting worry that the

magic might not work without all four Lights together, Rhianna laughed. "Oh stop it," she told the knights. "I grew up here, remember? If they wanted to hurt me, they could have done so a hundred times already while I was small, and I didn't even have a sword back then!"

"You had Elphin, though, didn't you?" Arianrhod reminded her.

Rhianna's heart tugged again.

"I've still got Elphin," she said firmly. "And I've got the Grail now, too! I can always use it to heal him as well as my father, if I need to."

Only then did she remember Lady Nimue's warning that the magic would only work once.

Her friends looked at her doubtfully.

"Will the magic work on an Avalonian?" Arianrhod asked.

"I don't know," Rhianna admitted. She managed another smile. "Let's not worry about that until we have to. Lord Avallach always holds a feast when he has visitors from the land of men, and you haven't seen a real feast until you've been to one in Avalon!"

Cai cheered up immediately. "Will there be a lot of food?" he said. "Because I'm starving."

***

They settled Alba and Evenstar in the mist horse stables with buckets of oats sweetened by Avalonian honey. Rhianna gave Mordred's rotting fist to Cai and ordered him to look after it. Then she allowed Arianrhod to dress her for the feast.

The Lady of Avalon had sent a beautiful green and gold gown for her to wear. The long skirt and low-cut bodice reminded Rhianna of the dresses her mother made her wear at Camelot. Thinking of her mother dressing for the feast in another part of the palace, she wondered what Sir Lancelot and Guinevere would do when King Arthur returned from the dead to reclaim his queen.

Two of the Avalonian girls brought wildflower crowns for her and Arianrhod. They ran their fingers over the dented cup Rhianna had set carefully on the bed.

"Is that really the Grail of Stars?" one asked in a disappointed tone. "It looks so ordinary."

"I can't feel any magic in it," said the other.

"Bet she's brought the wrong cup – how would a human with no magic know?"

"Leave that alone!" Arianrhod snapped. "Lady Rhia... *Princess* Rhianna's gone to a lot of trouble to get it. You've no idea what you're talking about."

"Oooh, we've no idea about magic, have we?" the first girl said in a teasing tone. "Would you like us to show you some?" She wriggled her six fingers and smirked at the maid. "Hand me Elphin's harp and I'll give you a lesson."

"It's got a broken string," Rhianna reminded them, too tired to play their games. "I only came back here to wake my father, and then we're leaving again."

"Oh yes?" The girls grinned at each other. "You're leaving with Prince Elphin lying in our crystal caverns? We've seen the way you look at him, and that's before he followed you to the land of men and nearly got himself killed for you. We know why you came back, *Princess*... and it's not for your father's sake!"

Her thoughts spinning in confusion, Rhianna rested her hand on Excalibur. "Go and see if my mother needs anything," she said. They ran off, giggling.

Arianrhod bit her lip and picked up one of the flower crowns. "I'm afraid you'll have to wear one of these tonight, Rhia," she said, "since the shadrake took the Crown of Dreams."

Rhianna unclenched her fist. "That's all right," she said with a smile. "They're pretty, and I want my father to see me looking like a princess when he wakes up."

Arianrhod smiled back. "You must look beautiful for Prince Elphin when he wakes, too!" she said, braiding Rhianna's bright hair around the scented petals.

Again, the confusion. Rhianna couldn't think of a suitable reply. She strapped Excalibur over the gown and told Arianrhod to bring the Grail.

"Let's get this over with," she said.

⚜

Lord Avallach's palace glittered with the light of a thousand candles. Dancers whirled under the crystal dome, while deer grazed outside the crystal walls, flickering in and out of the trees. At the far side of the hall, Queen Guinevere sat on a flower-wreathed dais with the Avalonian lord and his lady, looking around in a daze.

Rhianna watched impatiently as the stars came out one by one. She felt sick with nerves as she watched the dancers circling to the Avalonian music. The harpists reminded her of Elphin. She should have gone down to the crystal caverns with his body, instead of coming to the feast. What if she couldn't get past the enchantments, even carrying the fourth Light? What if her father's body had not healed properly?

Worse, what if she did something wrong and the magic did not work at all?

The knights stood awkwardly near the tables, keeping an eye on their queen and watching the Avalonians dance. They had taken off their armour in honour of the feast, but still wore their muddy boots with the rather short robes Lord Avallach had provided. They reminded Rhianna of Merlin before he lost his human form, when he'd brought the dying King Arthur from the battle and attended Lord Avallach's feast in borrowed clothes too small for him. She'd been angry with her father's druid at the time. She had grown up a lot since then.

Sir Bedivere brought her a skewer of mushrooms dripping with butter. "You have to eat something, Damsel Rhianna," he said, pushing it into her hand. "You haven't had a proper meal since Camelot."

The thought of eating made her feel sick. She shook her head. "I'll have to go down to the Moon Pool soon. It's nearly time." She checked Arianrhod still had the Grail safe, and glanced at the dais where her mother sat.

"I'm sure King Arthur will wait a bit longer," Sir Bedivere said with a smile. "He's waited this long… Er, is his ghost here now?"

Rhianna frowned. She must be tired. She'd forgotten to check on King Arthur's soul again. Where had it gone after they reached Avalon? He had ridden behind her on Alba while she played Lady Nimue's riddle game.

But she hadn't seen him since he'd left her to meet the Hunt on the beach. He'd promised to meet her tonight, but she couldn't see him in the banqueting hall. Had he followed the Avalonians, when they took Elphin down to the crystal caverns?

"Where are Sir Galahad and Sir Percival?" she asked.

"They stayed with the ship," Sir Bedivere told her. "Said they couldn't come to Avalon, something to do with the Wild Hunt taking their souls."

Rhianna smiled, remembering what her father's ghost had said about not tempting Lord Avallach's hunt. "He might have stayed with them, I suppose."

"Maybe he's already waiting down with his body, Rhia?" Arianrhod said.

Cai nodded. "She's right. That's where I'd go, if I was a ghost. Can we come down to the crystal caverns with you, Damsel Rhianna? The other boys back at Camelot will never believe half of this, when I tell them."

"They're not going to believe their eyes when King Arthur returns from the dead, that's for sure – though Gareth's friends seem happy enough with the idea," Sir Bedivere said with a smile, looking at the squires who were devouring the food at the far end of the hall. "Enjoy yourselves for a bit. Lancelot's got some kind of plan for our return home, and he wants to talk to us all before King Arthur wakes up."

Rhianna frowned as Sir Bedivere rejoined the others. If the knights were having a meeting about her father, she ought to be there – but she could not miss moonrise at the pool.

Cai eyed the dripping skewer in her hand. "Are you going to eat that?" She passed it to him, distracted, and he grinned at her as he slurped off the mushrooms. "So when do we go?" he asked, licking his lips.

"Now," she decided. "We'll go now."

"Hadn't you better tell Lord Avallach and the queen?" Arianrhod said, glancing at the crystal thrones.

She shook her head. "Lord Avallach will know. He always knows what's going on in his own land. And I don't want my mother there when I use the Grail."

✵

It was easy enough to slip away from the feast. Rhianna remembered the palace better than she'd hoped. She paused to collect her boots, then led Arianrhod and Cai out through a back door and down a winding path through the orchard, past the mist horse stables.

The moon was rising by the time they reached the pool. Stars reflected in the clear water. A waterfall rushed down the cliffs from the palace, shimmering with silver light. Rhianna thought of the waterfall that guarded the shadrake's lair where Mordred had held her captive last year, and stared at the foaming curtain, her heart quickening.

"What's wrong, Rhia?" Arianrhod whispered.

"Nothing. I just realised there might be another way into the crystal caverns, that's all. We won't have to go back up to the palace."

Cai followed her gaze and grinned. "Like in Dragonland, you mean? I think you're right

– there's a path behind the waterfall! I can see it from here."

"Shouldn't we take a guide?" Arianrhod said.

"No," Rhianna said firmly. She took Nimue's cup from the maid and dipped it into the pool. As she lifted it out, dripping, the Grail glittered silver too.

"The Grail of Stars," Arianrhod breathed. "It's true what the song says... look, it holds all the stars in Heaven!"

"They're just a reflection of the sky, silly," Cai said. But as he stared into the cup as well, a strange expression came over his face.

Rhianna felt dizzy. She shook her head to clear it, and quickly handed the full cup back to Arianrhod. Then she hitched up her skirts and led the way around the pool, on to the path behind the glimmering wall of water. Her heart beat faster. A tunnel led deep into the hill beneath Lord Avallach's palace. But rather than being dark rock, like the shadrake's lair that led to the gate of Annwn, this tunnel had a high roof that glittered with rainbows. Deep inside the hill, they could hear faint echoes of music from the feast above.

"It's so beautiful, Lady Rhia!" Arianrhod breathed. "When I die, I wouldn't mind being buried in here."

Rhianna gritted her teeth as sweat broke out under her dress. Beautiful or not, they still had to go underground, and this time Elphin was not here with his harp to chase away her terror. But Mordred was not waiting inside to chain her in the dark as he had been in Dragonland, she told herself firmly. His spirit was on its way to Annwn with the shadrake, hopefully this time for good.

"Bring the Grail, Arianrhod," she ordered. "Don't spill any of the water – we might need all of it. Cai, you stay out here and keep watch."

"But—" the boy protested.

"Stay!" Rhianna insisted. "Make sure nobody follows us inside. The last thing I need is an audience when I wake my father."

Cai scowled. "How come Arianrhod gets to see your magic caverns, and I don't?"

"Because she's a Grail maiden, and you're my champion," Rhianna said. "Arianrhod can't fight off the shadrake if it returns and tries to follow us in here. You've got the Lance of Truth, so you can."

Cai pulled a face and muttered something about there being nobody left to fight. But he took up position behind the waterfall with the Lance of Truth, guarding the entrance to the caves.

Rhianna drew Excalibur, made sure Arianrhod was following, and stepped into the tunnel.

◁ 13 ▷

Crystal Caverns

In crystal caves the king did sleep
Where souls of men come down to weep.
One last choice must our damsel make
To name the hero who will wake.

"Stay close behind me," Rhianna said, glancing round to check Arianrhod still had the Grail. "Don't look at the rainbows."

This was easier said than done. The colours rippled around them, shimmering at the mouths of hidden tunnels. The music echoed strangely as they ventured deeper into the caverns, and the sweet air made Rhianna dizzy. The tunnel they were following twisted and turned until she lost all sense of direction. Her skirt kept snagging on rocks, and she wished she'd stopped to change before they left the palace. She hoped they would be able to find the way out again afterwards with her father. He was sure to be weak and confused when he woke up.

"There are ghosts in here, Rhia," Arianrhod whispered, her voice tight with fear. "They're watching us."

"Don't look at them," Rhianna advised, raising Excalibur to light their way.

She too had noticed the faces shifting and blurring in the crystal walls. They reached out to her and Arianrhod as they passed, wailing, *"Me! Choose me!"*

Rhianna shuddered. But at least these caverns weren't dark, and they didn't smell as bad as the shadrake's lair. Gradually her sweat eased. She looked more closely at the ghosts in the walls, searching for her father's face. But she didn't recognise any of them.

"They must be waiting for their bodies to heal," Arianrhod said. "I wonder how long they've been down here?"

Rhianna hated to think. She paused again to listen to the music. "Come on, I think we're beneath the palace now. Let's try this way."

They took another turn, and the tunnel emerged halfway up a huge cavern filled with glittering crystal caskets from floor to roof. These appeared to be floating in midair. Magical walkways twisted between them, drifting about the cavern – ribbons of light that reminded Rhianna of Merlin's spiral path. She looked down past her toes and watched one of the pathways rise up slowly from a haze of rainbows to join the end of their tunnel. She sucked in her breath and stepped quickly back into the tunnel to make room for it as it closed the gap. Arianrhod trod on her heels, and cold liquid splashed across Rhianna's neck.

The maid gasped. "Oh, I'm sorry my lady!"

While the pathway settled into place, Rhianna anxiously checked the grail, her heart thumping. Half of the precious Moon Pool water had spilled.

Arianrhod held the cup out to her, shaking. "I nearly dropped it," she whispered. "You take it now, Rhia, please. I can't carry it out *there*."

"I can't carry the Grail as well as my sword," Rhianna said firmly. "You're doing fine.

My father's body must be in here somewhere. Follow me, and don't look down."

Taking a deep breath, she hitched up her skirt and stepped carefully out on to the shining pathway. It swayed a little, but she gripped Excalibur tighter and strode confidently down the gentle slope through the maze of caskets, peering through the crystal lids. She heard Arianrhod's frightened breathing close behind her. But as they slowly descended, the maid gained courage and ventured along more of the magical paths to check on the other caskets. Each time, she returned shaking her head.

Rhianna wondered if they would have to search the entire cavern. The moving pathways made her dizzy, and she had no idea how they were going to get back out again. But as they neared the floor of the cavern, she saw a shadowy ghost sitting on a large casket below. He looked old and tired and strangely familiar, though he wasn't her father – at least not the way she remembered him. She put a finger to her lips. Excalibur's blade gleamed brighter as they crept down the rest of the way. She and Arianrhod stepped off the path, and it vanished behind them in a glitter of stars.

She pushed Arianrhod behind her as the ghost rose to his feet and shuffled across the polished floor to meet them, leaning on a ghostly staff. He had falcon feathers braided into a long silver beard and pale blue eyes.

"You took your time, Rhianna Pendragon, I must say!" he grumbled. "Put that sword away – there's no one to fight in here. I've been waiting for you."

"Merlin!" Arianrhod gasped, slopping more water from the Grail.

"Don't drop that thing, girl!" Merlin told the trembling maid. "We've all been through enough trouble to get it here."

Rhianna kept Excalibur in her hand and watched the druid warily. "How did you get out of the shadrake's body when Mordred took it over?" she asked.

Merlin's eyes twinkled. "Same way I got into it, of course. The spirit transfer is not difficult for a druid. When you told the creature to take Mordred to Annwn, I knew it was time for me to leave. The problem can be finding another convenient body, but it wasn't too hard this time – I hitched a ride here with Elphin's horse."

"Evenstar!" Rhianna said, remembering the

little horse bucking on the beach. "No wonder he was so panicky when he galloped past me."

"Mmm," Merlin said. "Mist horses don't take kindly to being spirit-ridden. But he'll forget his experience soon enough, and in this place I can take my original form to talk to you. My old body is down here too somewhere. Nimue's people rescued it from the Summer Sea and brought it here after I was forced to abandon it, but I'm afraid it'll be some time before it recovers from Morgan Le Fay's mischief."

It seemed a lifetime since Mordred's mother had ambushed Rhianna and Elphin as Merlin guided them through the mists at the start of her quest. Did that mean the druid would return to his old body one day and rejoin King Arthur at Camelot, like in all the songs?

She peered hopefully through the rainbows at the glimmering pathways, but could see nobody using them, living or dead. "Where's my father's soul?" she asked. "Is he down here with you?"

"He'll be here soon enough now the Grail has arrived, not to worry." Merlin frowned slightly and peered into the cup Arianrhod held. "I just hope it'll be enough," he muttered, dipping his finger into the water and licking it. "You could have stolen a bigger cup."

Thinking of Lady Nimue's warning about the magic only working once, Rhianna snatched the Grail from Arianrhod before Merlin could taste any more of its contents. She scowled at him.

"Where's King Arthur's casket?" she demanded. "Because I brought this Grail to wake my father, not you. What have you done to him?"

She looked around the cavern again, suddenly suspicious. Merlin and Mordred had been in the shadrake's body together plenty long enough to plot a final betrayal.

"Nothing Mordred didn't do," Merlin said. "In this place, we take the form closest to our original bodies, and Arthur was mortally wounded at Camlann as you know. But he'll be fine when you use the Grail to wake him. I expect he's keeping an eye on Guinevere and Lancelot up there – our two love birds will need to be a bit more discreet when Arthur returns." He chuckled. "Besides, whatever makes you think I want my old body back? I, Merlin, last of the druids, who has flown with dragons and seen the world through the keen eyes of a falcon! No thank you, Rhianna Pendragon. You're not getting me back into that creaking old carcass that needs a staff just to walk! I've a mind to hang around these pretty caves of Avallach's for a while, until something better comes along."

Rhianna wondered what 'something better' might be, after spirit-riding a dragon. Then she saw her father's druid smile and had another chilling thought. What if he meant a younger, stronger body? One that could work magic better than his old one?

"Have you seen Elphin?" she asked, wary again. "The Avalonians brought him down here, earlier."

But Merlin shook his head. "Don't get distracted, Rhianna Pendragon. Your father's body is this way. Come." He led the way back across the cavern towards the casket he had been sitting on.

She hesitated.

"I'll look for Elphin's casket, Rhia," Arianrhod whispered. "You go ahead and wake your father. I'm sure King Arthur won't want to see my ugly face when he opens his eyes." She touched her scarred cheek self-consciously.

"You're not ugly, Arianrhod," Rhianna said, frowning. "That scar Lady Morgan gave you only makes the rest of you look prettier." But she gave her friend a grateful smile as she hurried after the druid.

As they approached the large casket, Rhianna saw its crystal lid had been inlaid with gold. Around it, several other beautiful caskets formed a circle – some of them empty, the rest occupied by her father's slain knights.

Rhianna's heart pounded as she joined the druid. Her palms began to sweat. She clutched the Grail tighter, afraid it would slip through her fingers.

Beneath the crystal lid, on a bed of white silk, her father's body lay exactly as she remembered it from Merlin's boat, when the druid had brought the dying king to Avalon straight from the battlefield. The king's chestnut hair, streaked with grey, fanned out around his head. His strong hands were folded on his breast, over the death wound Mordred had dealt him, and his boots still had mud on them, crumbling now to dust.

Tears filled Rhianna's eyes. The mud might have dried. But what she could see of his wound looked just as bad as before. Blood spotted the white silk of his casket, and his skin was deathly pale.

Anger filled her. "I thought you said these caverns would heal him?" she said, rounding on Merlin. "He looks worse than he did when you brought him here after the battle!"

Merlin grunted. "It takes time to heal a body wounded as badly as Arthur's. Much of the initial healing happens on the inside. I think he'll recover enough for our purposes, once you use the Grail to restore his soul. We only need him to sit on his throne to show the Saxons and northern tribes that Camelot has a king again. He doesn't have to fight."

"But I can't send my father's soul back into *that*!" Rhianna said in horror, looking at the body in the casket. "He'll suffer when he wakes up!"

"Probably," the druid agreed. "But he'll be alive. That's what you want, isn't it?"

Rhianna looked into the cup she held. The water in the bottom seemed less bright than before.

She frowned. "I want my father to carry Excalibur again and ride back to Camelot beside my mother! I want him to protect everyone from the dark knight…" she paused, remembering that she'd already defeated Prince Mordred, then finished, "… I want him to help me bring peace to the land of men."

Merlin was watching her. "So open your father's casket and give him the water from that grail you hold," he said. "I can't open it for you. I'm just a ghost in this place."

Rhianna set the cup down carefully on the cavern floor. She ran her fingers over the gold lettering on the lid. "What does it say?" she whispered, ashamed she still hadn't found the time to learn to read.

"It says, *Here Lies Arthur, Once and Future King of Men,*" Merlin told her.

Rhianna swallowed. Once and future king. Then her father *would* wake and be king of men again one day.

She bit her lip and looked round again for King Arthur's ghost. "Father?" she said. "Are you here? Are you ready to go back into your body now? Would you like me to wake you?"

A soft breeze blew through the caverns, rippling her skirt and making the magical pathways swirl overhead. But King Arthur's ghost still did not appear. Rhianna couldn't really blame it.

"Will the Grail heal his body, when his soul is restored?" she demanded of Merlin.

The druid shook his head. "I do not know, child. Give him the cup to drink from, and we'll find out. The fourth Light has the power to command any man's spirit back into its body, even an unwilling one."

"But what if the magic doesn't work?" she whispered.

"Rhianna Pendragon!" Merlin drew himself up to his full ghostly height. "I didn't teach you how to walk the spiral path, help you find the four Lights, and humiliate myself before Morgan Le Fay, to have you go all soft on me now! Do it quickly, before Lord Avallach comes down here and—"

"And what, Merlin?" an amused voice said from the rainbows behind them.

Rhianna whirled, almost knocking over the Grail. Her hand flew instinctively to her sword. But she slid Excalibur's blade back into its scabbard when she saw Lord Avallach had Arianrhod's wrist clasped in his six strong fingers.

She watched the Avalonian lord warily.

Arianrhod gave her an apologetic look. "I'm sorry, my lady," she whispered. "But he was already down here with Elphin's casket."

Rhianna's heart leaped. Elphin was near! She wanted to rush over and check on her friend. But she had to find out what had happened to her father's soul first. She kept her hand on Excalibur's hilt and her gaze on Lord Avallach. At least he hadn't brought her mother with him.

"*Faha'ruh*, Rhianna Pendragon," the Avalonian lord said formally. "So here you are at the end of your quest. And here's old

Merlin, come to make sure you do the right thing… yet the druid has never really belonged in either of our worlds, have you Merlin?" Lord Avallach turned his purple gaze on the druid's spirit. "Cai tells me you are the dark knight's father. Is this true?"

Merlin frowned. "I knew that boy's tongue would get someone in trouble one of these days," he muttered. "It was just one night in the druid grove. Morgan Le Fay had her charms. I was young, the witch was determined, and I paid for my mistake. I didn't even know for sure, until she told me the truth when Mordred captured my falcon's body. I kept my promise to my king. I brought the girl here with the Grail."

"And now she has a final choice to make," Lord Avallach said. He glanced sadly into King

Arthur's casket then rested his gaze on Rhianna. "I warned you before that your father's body was not healing as quickly as it should. Now you can see the truth with your own eyes. If you use that Grail you carry to wake him, he will live. But I can't guarantee he'll be riding his horse any time soon, perhaps never again. If you leave him down here, however, time will eventually heal his wounds, as it heals everything."

"How long?" Rhianna demanded, still gripping Excalibur.

Lord Avallach exchanged a glance with Merlin. "As long as it takes. A thousand of your years, maybe more."

Rhianna's heart twisted.

So Mordred had been right, after all! He had warned her at their very first meeting that her father would sleep for thousands of years –

and she hadn't believed him. She'd thought if she could just find the Grail of Stars, she could make everything right again. But of course the Lights must have their limits, too. Otherwise Mordred could never have killed King Arthur, who had been carrying the Sword of Light and wearing the Crown of Dreams when the two of them fought at Camlann.

She took a deep breath and made herself look at her father's wounded body. "And then he'll be strong again? Healed properly?"

Lord Avallach nodded. "As strong as he was before the battle with Mordred. Stronger."

"But I won't be alive to see him when he wakes up, will I?" she said, finally realising the price she would pay. "Or my mother? Or his champion, Sir Lancelot, or any of the knights up there in your hall?"

"That's right," Merlin said quickly. "You, your mother, and Arthur's faithful knights will all have grown old and died long before that. If you want to take your father home to Camelot, you know what you need to do."

In the silence that followed his words, Rhianna could not think straight.

"Elphin will still be here when King Arthur wakes," Arianrhod whispered. "Avalonians don't die, do they?"

Rhianna gave her friend a distracted look. But Lord Avallach smiled at the girl. "Your maid is quite right. And we can bring the rest of Arthur's knights down here to sleep with their king when they die." He indicated the empty caskets. "I've already got spaces waiting for Sir Lancelot, Sir Bors, Sir Agravaine and Sir Bedivere, and I can easily make one for young Sir Cai... Arthur won't wake alone. When he calls on their spirits, his knights will wake to ride with him again."

Rhianna wet her lips. "And what about me? Can I have a casket down here too, when I die?"

Lord Avallach smiled at her. "We don't usually bring damsels down here. But from what I've heard, you're as heroic as any of your father's knights, so I'll make an exception in your case, if you still want that when your time comes. You don't have to decide now. You have your whole life ahead of you, even if it's only a short human span. I'm sure your father would want you to enjoy that life first."

Rhianna looked into the Grail and saw her own reflection staring back. She still wore her wildflower crown, wilting a little now.

"A thousand years is such a long time…" she whispered.

"Don't be silly, Rhianna Pendragon!" Merlin snapped. "You don't have to wait nearly that long. You've got the Grail of Stars! At least give its magic a try, before you let Camelot's glory fade. I'm sure your father would prefer to sit on his throne again as a cripple, beside his queen, than wait a thousand years and start over with new tribes of barbarians to conquer."

"It's Rhianna's Grail," Lord Avallach said firmly. "Only she can decide how to use it. I've already explained this to the queen, who says the same as I do."

Rhianna nodded, her decision made. "I want my father to wake whole and strong again, however long that takes. "He's going to need the Sword of Light to call the souls of his knights back into their bodies when he does."

She unbuckled Excalibur from her waist and stroked the white jewel on the hilt. Then she lifted the lid of her father's casket and gently pushed the Sword between his clasped hands so that it lay over his heart, hiding the wound. "Maybe the magic will help heal him if he sleeps with the strength of a hundred knights in his hands," she added. She quickly closed the lid again before she could change her mind.

"Thank you, daughter," said her father's voice in her ear.

She spun round in sudden hope.

King Arthur's ghost stood behind Merlin's, looking very solid and strong as he rested a hand on the druid's shoulder. His blue eyes crinkled as he smiled at Rhianna. "I do believe I feel better already," he said.

Warmth filled her. She looked into the casket and saw the king's wounds were closing. She smiled her father's soul in relief. "Then you don't mind waiting a bit longer for your body to heal properly?"

King Arthur's soul smiled again. "Not at all. Time runs differently here in Avalon, and you deserve some happiness of your own after ridding the world of Prince Mordred. Lancelot will look after Guinevere until he joins me down here. Let the child alone, Merlin. She's brought me back my sword. She's done better than you deserve."

Arianrhod clasped her hands together, her eyes wet with tears. Lord Avallach squeezed the maid's shoulder and said, "Don't be sad.

Your princess has made a good choice."

Merlin sat on the king's casket and dropped his head in his hands. "I knew it," he grumbled. "I *knew* the girl would do something like this... Why couldn't Guinevere have had a son I could have trained from an early age, instead of a daughter who was allowed to grow up wild, riding fairy horses? You might as well pour that magic water away, Rhianna Pendragon! I can see you're not going to be happy until you get your father back to Camelot as strong as he was before, and bring peace to the entire land of men while you're at it! Just don't expect me to help you. I'm going to rest down here for a while. I'm tired. Take that Grail of yours out of here. It's making my poor old spirit hurt."

He aimed a kick at Nimue's cup. Fortunately,

his ghostly foot passed right through it and the water inside only shivered.

Rhianna quickly rescued the Grail and its contents. Now she'd made up her mind, she felt much better. Her mother didn't really need King Arthur to come back from the dead, anyway, not now she had found happiness with Sir Lancelot – it would only have complicated things at Camelot.

Satisfied her father was happy with her decision, Rhianna looked at Arianrhod. "It'd be a shame to waste the Grail's magic," she said with a smile. "Wouldn't it?"

Arianrhod's face brightened. "Elphin's over here, my lady," she said, leading the way across the cavern.

Her friend lay in another beautiful crystal casket with golden writing on the lid. "It says *Here Lies Elphin, Crown Prince of Avalon*," Arianrhod informed her, before Rhianna could ask. The maid glanced at Lord Avallach for permission before opening the casket.

A lump caught in Rhianna's throat. Elphin looked so peaceful, as if he'd just fallen asleep. But she could see the green blisters around his wrists left by Mordred's enchanted ropes. She knelt beside the casket, cradled her friend's head in her arm and carefully lowered the Grail of Stars to his lips. The water sparkled as it entered his mouth.

For two heartbeats, nothing happened. She wondered if she'd chosen the wrong Grail, after all, and a great sadness filled her. Would everyone she loved sleep here in Lord Avallach's crystal caverns until she was long dead?

Then the wind came again, stirring her hair and sending petals down on to the body she cradled. Elphin spluttered and coughed, and his eyes opened. He stared up at Rhianna with eyes full of violet light, and she felt his spirit shiver as the enchantment left him. The marks on his wrists faded.

He lifted a six-fingered hand to touch the cup in wonder. Then he smiled and tweaked her messy braid. "You found it, then," he said. "I knew you would. Have I missed much?"

Rhianna grinned. "Only a visit to the Grail Castle, a battle against Uther Pendragon's ghost-army at the Lonely Tor, sending the shadrake off with Prince Mordred's spirit to join his witch-mother's in Annwn, and Queen Guinevere coming to Avalon in disguise," she said. "Oh, and a long argument with your father about raising King Arthur from the dead."

"Don't forget Merlin spirit-riding Evenstar!" Arianrhod added with a giggle. "That was funny."

Elphin blinked, his violet gaze still fixed on Rhianna's face. "So now you've defeated Prince Mordred and woken your father, I suppose you're going home to Camelot to live happily ever after?"

Rhianna laughed. "Not quite yet," she said quickly, before Arianrhod could launch into an explanation of King Arthur sleeping in his casket for the next thousand years. "I've got one more thing to do first."

"What's that?" Elphin asked, sitting up.

"This!" She seized Elphin's tangled curls in

both hands, pulled his head towards her and kissed him firmly on the lips.

◄◄ 14 ►►

The Quest Ends

Against the dark four Lights will stand
When elfin fire burns Mordred's hand.
One under crystal, one out of sight,
One for the dragon, one with a knight.

When Elphin felt strong enough, they made their way back into the main cavern to find Lord Avallach. Rhianna hesitated as they passed her father's glittering casket, where King Arthur's soul was sitting beside Merlin's ghost. But her father smiled when he saw her with the Avalonian boy. "Have a good life, daughter," he said, rising easily to his feet and opening his arms.

Rhianna let the ghost hug her. When she closed her eyes, he felt almost as strong as Sir Bors. A lump rose to her throat. "I'm sorry I failed my quest, Father," she whispered.

"You didn't fail, daughter," he said. "It wasn't quite the same quest you thought it would be when you started out, that's all. I feel much stronger now you've returned Excalibur to me, so I'll be able to visit you more often in future. Now go! This is no place for the living." He gently lifted the flower crown off her head and gave her a little push. As Rhianna rejoined her friends, he called, "Look after my daughter, Prince Elphin! I'll be keeping an eye on you."

"Better warn your daughter to look after

my son, more like!" Lord Avallach called back. King Arthur grinned, and Merlin shook his head in defeat.

They left the two ghosts in the crystal rainbows, discussing old times. With Lord Avallach's help, their route out of the caverns was much quicker than going in. He simply pulled down one of the shining pathways with a six-fingered hand and commanded it to carry them into the upper levels. He paused at a flight of steps that led up to his palace to give Rhianna and Elphin an amused look. "I expect you youngsters would like a bit of time alone. I'll tell your mother and her knights you'll meet them at the ship. Stay with your mistress, Arianrhod, or tongues will wag."

Rhianna blushed. She led the way back along the tunnel towards the waterfall, thinking of

what her father had said. Not the same quest...
if it hadn't been to bring her father back to
Camelot, then what else had she done, besides
finding all four Lights? She'd already lost one
of them to the dragon, and was supposed to
return the fourth to Queen Nimue.

Before they reached the exit, a shadow
loomed against the glimmering water. She felt
for her sword, forgetting she'd left Excalibur in
King Arthur's casket. She pushed Arianrhod
and Elphin back, prepared to use the empty
Grail as a weapon if need be.

A glittering lance head poked around the
bend. "Stop right there, whoever you are!"
called a shaky voice.

"Cai!" Rhianna said in relief. "It's us, you
dolt. What are you doing down here? I thought
I told you to wait outside."

The lance rattled against the rock, and Cai's head appeared in its place. "Damsel Rhianna!" he scolded. "You've been *ages* – it's almost sunrise. Did you wake King Arthur?" He peered behind her, saw Elphin and grinned. "Welcome back to the land of the living, fairy boy!"

"Watch who you're calling a fairy, squire," Elphin said. "You're in my world now remember."

"Watch who you're calling a squire," Cai replied in kind. "You wouldn't be here at all if I hadn't helped get Damsel Rhia out of the Grail Castle."

"None of us would be here if I hadn't swapped the Grails," Arianrhod said with surprising confidence. She pushed past Rhianna and took Cai's arm, pulling him out of the way. "Shut your mouth for once, Cai, and let Princess Rhia keep her promise to the fish-queen."

Rhianna smiled. Leaving Arianrhod to explain about King Arthur's body not being healed enough yet to wake, she hurried out through the waterfall. Dawn was breaking over the sea. Had they been in Lord Avallach's crystal caverns that long? She clutched the empty cup, suddenly nervous. What if Lady Nimue thought she'd broken her promise and ordered her fish-people to stop the ship returning them to the world of men?

But as they stood watching the mist brighten, a tail splashed in the pool and the fish-queen surfaced.

Nimue gave Elphin a long look and smiled at Rhianna. "The Grail worked for you, I see," she said. "So now your quest is over, Rhianna Pendragon, and it's time the Lights returned to their proper homes to restore the balance in the world. The Sword will stay with Arthur in Avalon, where it was forged. The Crown is on its way to Annwn, and the Lance is back in the hands of men – or a boy's, anyway."

She gave Cai, who was standing close to Arianrhod, an amused look. "Though it seems he's claimed one of my maidens, so I suppose the boy shall soon enough grow into a man. That leaves just one exchange to be made. You have my Grail, and I have something of yours. I rescued it from the sea when it fell out of the shadrake's pouch."

She opened her webbed hand to reveal a glinting silver spiral.

"Merlin's pathfinder!" Rhianna remembered

the falling treasure when Merlin and Mordred had been fighting for control of the shadrake's body. She'd been starting to wonder how they would get back through the mists to the land of men without it.

"This will be rather more use to your Avalonian friend than it is to me," Nimue said, holding out the pathfinder for Elphin to take.

He reached warily across the water and snatched the little spiral from the fish-lady's webbed hand.

Nimue gave a tinkling laugh. "Relax, Prince Elphin! The one Rhianna chose to wake has nothing to fear from me. But use it wisely when you visit the land of men. I have a feeling they will soon forget the old ways, now Merlin and Arthur no longer walk among them. My cup, Rhianna Pendragon?"

Rhianna wrenched her gaze from Elphin and tossed the Grail to Lady Nimue. It flashed in the first rays of the rising sun, dazzling them all. The fish-lady caught it easily.

"Thank you," Nimue said. "Have a good voyage home, and don't forget to burn Mordred's mortal remains before you leave. The shadrake has flown to Annwn with the dark knight's spirit, and we don't want him coming back again to disturb the balance of the world – not after we've worked so hard to restore it." Her tail splashed once, and then she was gone.

Rhianna took a deep breath. So her quest had helped to rebalance the world! But she had almost forgotten Mordred's dark fist. She turned to Cai. "I don't suppose you brought the gauntlet down here…?"

The boy shook his head. "It stank to high

heaven. I left it on the ship with Sir Galahad and Sir Percival."

"Then we've got to get to the jetty as fast as possible." She looked at the nearby mist horse stables and grinned at Elphin. "Race?"

※

As she mounted Alba bareback, Rhianna's heart beat faster. Arianrhod clung nervously to her waist, while Cai climbed up on Evenstar behind Elphin.

They cantered through the sun-dappled wood, both mist horses on their best behaviour because they carried humans who would fall off if they misted around trees. The ride reminded Rhianna of their childhood races, before she'd discovered she was King Arthur's daughter. She ducked the golden branches, laughing when

Arianrhod gasped and clutched her waist. It felt strange to be riding in a skirt, but she quite liked the feel of Alba's warm coat against her bare legs.

They found the knights arguing loudly on the jetty. Queen Guinevere stood nearby, wearing her travelling cloak and staring anxiously at the path through the wood. Rhianna heard her name mentioned and King Arthur's. But when they saw the mist horses coming, the men broke off their argument and strode to meet them.

"Did the Grail of Stars work, Princess?" Sir Lancelot asked gruffly, looking behind them for the king. "Old Avallach wouldn't tell us anything."

"It worked," Elphin said with a little smile.

"Then… King Arthur's coming back

with us?" Sir Bedivere asked, with a glance at Guinevere.

"Not yet." Rhianna looked at Elphin and blushed for the second time that morning. The knights frowned at them, not understanding. But the queen gave Rhianna a sharp look and smiled slightly under her hood.

Rhianna did not feel up to facing her mother yet. "You tell them, Arianrhod," she said, jumping off Alba to collect Mordred's dark fist from the ship. "We'll get the fire started."

Cai was right. The fist stank. When she thrust the gauntlet through her belt, it made a squelchy sound. She wondered if it would be too rotten to burn.

But when Elphin used magic to light the sticks Cai had gathered, the fire crackled fiercely. The branches from Avalon's golden wood burned with bright purple flames. The mist horses watched from a safe distance, ears pricked.

Back on the jetty, Rhianna could see the knights loading up the ship. They cast glances down the beach, where the queen sat on a rock to watch. But after what Arianrhod had told them, they obviously thought she was saying a tearful goodbye to her Avalonian friend and did not interfere.

She stared at Mordred's black gauntlet, remembering all the times it had gripped her wrist with its dark magic. "You've lost, Mordred," she said. "My father might not sit on the throne of Camelot, but you *never* will." She gritted her teeth and squeezed the fist as hard as she could. Pus sprayed her boots, making her jump.

"Steady, Rhia," Elphin said softly. "He can't hurt you now."

She grimaced and cast the gauntlet and its gruesome contents into the flames. The flames turned green as they ate the rotting leather. The fire hissed and spat, making them step back. The queen started down the beach towards them, and Lancelot hurried after her. The mist horses trotted away to a safer distance, whinnying in fear.

Cai gripped the Lance of Truth and stood guard between Arianrhod and the fire. Elphin hummed under his breath. Choking green smoke rose into the air to be blown away by the sweet Avalonian breeze, and the flames died.

Cai warily poked the ashes with his lance. "I think it's gone, Damsel Rhia," he said.

Rhianna pushed him aside and stamped

on the smouldering embers. With each stamp, she thought of Mordred's axe coming down on her father's head... her mother chained in the dark knight's tower... Arianrhod trapped in Camelot's dungeon... the shadrake attacking Cai... Elphin lying in his crystal casket.

"Never again, Mordred," she whispered, tears blurring her vision. "You'll never hurt my family or my friends again!"

"Rhia...?" Elphin touched her arm. "Rhia, Cai's right. He's gone, and you'll set fire to your dress if you're not careful. The knights saw that magic. Dry your eyes, they're coming."

She blinked away her tears and stared down at her singed boots, panting. She smoothed her skirt, caught her breath and turned to face her mother and Sir Lancelot. The other knights hurried up behind them, swords drawn. They watched the Avalonian prince warily.

"It's all right," Rhianna said, taking Elphin's six-fingered hand in hers and holding it tightly as she met her mother's gaze. "He was just testing his magic to make sure Mordred's enchantments haven't harmed it."

Sir Lancelot looked at the spiral pathfinder glinting around Elphin's neck. "Seems to work fine," he grunted. "So, fairy lad, are you coming back with us to take old Merlin's place at Camelot?"

Elphin looked at Rhianna, his violet eyes luminous. "I will if Rhia wants me to," he said.

Rhianna took a deep breath. "There's no need," she said, still watching her mother.

"You mean now Mordred's gone?" Sir Bors said, glancing at the others. "Yes, it's probably for the best if Prince Elphin stays here in

Avalon with his people. If you can just guide us through the mists as far as the Tor, lad, we'll make our own way back from there."

Arianrhod frowned at Rhianna and bit her lip. "She means there's no need for Elphin to take Merlin's place at Camelot, because she's not coming back with us – are you, Lady Rhia?" she whispered.

The queen nodded. Sir Bors turned red. Sir Agravaine scowled. Sir Bedivere started to tell her not to be so silly, of course Rhianna must come back with them.

But Sir Lancelot laughed. "I knew it," he said. "The pair of them are as besotted as me and Guinevere used to be when we were younger!"

The knights glanced at one another, a bit embarrassed. But when the queen smiled and said age had nothing to do with it, they chuckled too.

"We'll visit Camelot for all the feast days, Mother," Rhianna promised. "I release my maid Arianrhod so she can marry Cai if she likes. I'll look after my father's body, don't worry about that, and you can come over to Avalon to visit us sometimes, too…"

"Enough, Rhianna!" Guinevere said, drawing her into a flower-scented embrace. "It's all right, you know. Lord Avallach has explained everything. You must find your own happiness, and if your quest ends here in Avalon then so be it. You've rid us all of Mordred, that's the main thing. No mother could wish for a braver daughter. But I don't think you're entirely a lost cause as a princess, either – at least you're wearing a dress with your boots these days…" She released Rhianna and gave Elphin a mischievous look. "I'm just wondering how many fingers my grandchildren will have?"

Elphin's eyes gleamed violet. Rhianna blushed furiously, and everyone laughed.

Dark Gate

"Mother!" Mordred screamed as the shadrake crashed through the Gate of Annwn, shattering the Crown of Dreams into a million pieces and releasing his spirit into the void.

He became aware of other disembodied spirits wailing around him, the souls of all the men he had killed. He screamed again as they reached for him with their ghostly green hands. Whenever one of them touched him, he felt his crippled body around him again, along with all its old pains.

"MOTHER!" Mordred yelled again.

He thought she couldn't hear him. Then the witch's spirit appeared in a twist of dark smoke.

"I warned you to look after your mortal fist!" she snapped. "But you let the girl take it. And now she's destroyed your final link to the world of men. I can't help you any more."

"But… can't you send me back as a ghost, like Grandpa Uther and his men?" Mordred begged. "We can ambush Arthur and his daughter in the mists before they get halfway to Camelot, and—"

The witch hissed. "Foolish boy! Have you learned *nothing* about spirit magic after all these years? The shadrake has destroyed the Crown of Dreams! Without it, there's no one I know who has the power to summon your soul back through the dark gate. Besides,

Arthur is not yet awake so will lie safely in Lord Avallach's crystal caverns for some time to come."

These words found their way through Mordred's pain. "B-but I thought Rhianna found the Grail of Stars!" he said in confusion. "Didn't its magic work, then? Didn't she use it to wake her father?"

His final hope faded – that he would somehow escape from this place, get the Grail off his cousin, and use it to raise himself from the dead.

The witch laughed, a mad cackle. "She tricked us all, my son. Our brave damsel used the Grail all right, but not in the way anyone expected, not even old Merlin. Lancelot sits on the throne of Camelot beside Queen Guinevere, while Arthur heals in Avalon.

The Lights have returned to their makers, as Nimue must have intended all along."

She gave him a look that chilled his spirit.

"We've failed, my son. The balance of power is restored, and the gate of Annwn is shut. Rhianna and her friends have won."

ABOUT THE AUTHOR

Katherine Roberts' muse is a unicorn.
This is what he has to say about her...

My author has lived in King Arthur's country for most of her life. She went to Bath University, where she got a degree in Maths and learned to fly in a glider. Afterwards she worked with racehorses, until she found me in 1984 and wrote her first fantasy story. She won the Branford Boase Award in 2000 with her first book *Song Quest*, and has had me hard at work ever since, seeking out more magical stories for her to write.

www.katherineroberts.co.uk

 @AuthorKatherine   @PendragonGirl

'Weaves Arthurian
legend, Celtic myth
and imagination into
a romping tale.'
The Times

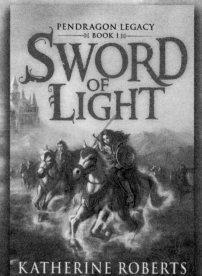

Available now!
PENDRAGON LEGACY
BOOKS 1 — 3

It is the darkest hour of the darkest age.

King Arthur is dead and the path to the throne lies open to his evil nephew, Mordred.

But there is one with a better claim...

Introducing Rhianna Pendragon: Arthur's secret daughter and Camelot's last hope.